PRAISE FOR SID

"*Sid* is a magical read, sweet, sad, beautiful. A haunting Zen imagining of the Buddha's life and our own."
—James Ishmael Ford, author of *If You're Lucky, Your Heart Will Break*

"Maybe three times in my life I've wept at the sheer beauty of a book. This is one of those times. *Sid* is deep spiritual teaching clothed as a contemporary retelling of the story of the Buddha. There is heartbreak. There is humor. There is joy. There is aliveness and compassion. And there is love, great love. I bow to the ground in gratitude."
—Geri Larkin, author of *Close to the Ground*

"Feng tells us a story in luminous prose-poem paragraphs about an ordinary contemporary high school math teacher whose journey parallels the Buddha's. *Sid* reminds me that I, too, ordinary as I am, have Buddha nature, and that my seeking is not in vain."
—Susan Moon, coeditor of *The Hidden Lamp*

SID

SID

Anita N. Feng

Wisdom

Wisdom Publications
199 Elm Street
Somerville, MA 02144 USA
wisdompubs.org

Library of Congress Cataloging-in-Publication Data
Feng, Anita, 1952–
 Sid / Anita Feng.
   pages ; cm
 ISBN 978-1-61429-227-2 (softcover : acid-free paper) — ISBN 1-61429-
227-2 (softcover : acid-free paper) — ISBN 978-1-61429-242-5 (ebook)
 1. Spiritual life—Buddhism—Fiction. 2. Enlightenment (Buddhism)—
Fiction. 3. Buddhism—Fiction. I. Title.
 PS3556.E4774S55 2015
 813'.54—dc23

                         2015000048

ISBN 978-1-61429-227-2
ebook ISBN 978-1-61429-242-5

19 18 17 16 15
 5 4 3 2 1

Artwork by Linda Davidson.
Cover and interior design by Katrina Noble. Set in Sina 9/14 & Futura Std.

Wisdom Publications' books are printed on acid-free paper and meet the
guidelines for permanence and durability of the Production Guidelines for
Book Longevity of the Council on Library Resources.

This book was produced with environmental mindfulness. We have elected
to print this title on 30% PCW recycled paper. As a result, we have saved
the following resources: 4 trees, 2 million BTUs of energy, 343 lbs. of green-
house gases, 1,858 gallons of water, and 125 lbs. of solid waste. For more
information, please visit our website, wisdompubs.org.

Printed in the United States of America.

Please visit fscus.org.

In memory of my father, Jacob Stern.

In gratitude for my teachers, Buddha, Bodhidharma,
Ma-tsu, Lin-Chi, Zen Master Seung Sahn, Zen Master Ji Bong,
rabbit, and crow.

TABLE OF CONTENTS

CAST OF CHARACTERS

Avalokiteśvara / Ava	*The bodhisattva of compassion, also known as Guan Yin, Kwan Seum Bosal, Kannon, etc.; Midwife and nanny to Sid and Siddhārtha; Nanny to Rāhula; Student of Sid; Spokesperson for the women of Kapilavastu*
Buddah	*Proprietor of the salvage yard*
Crow, Rabbit, Bear, Hawk, Trees, Cosmos	*Sentient beings*
Gossips	*Hungry Ghosts*
Homeless Woman	*Old age, sickness, and death*
Mahāmāyā	*Mother of Siddhārtha*
Maya	*Mother of Sid*

Passengers	*You and me*
Professor Sudovsky	*Father of Sid*
King Śuddhodana	*Father of Siddhārtha*
Rāhula	*Son of Sid and Siddhārtha*
Sid	*Sid Sudovsky*
Siddhārtha	*Siddhārtha Gautama*
Yasmin	*Wife of Sid*
Yaśodhara	*Wife of Siddhārtha*
Buddha	*All of the Above*

BIRTH

KAPILAVASTU
The Himalayan foothills, Nepal, 5th c. BCE

Ask anyone and they will tell you that Kapilavastu is built out of a fragment of sky mixed with a bit of Tuṣita heaven. The city walls spread thick like clouds of buttery light, and every house within exudes a splendor that even its residents can't quite believe. Precious stones litter the paths. Precious blossoms embroider the trees. Within the city's magnificent gates, darkness is as alien as a hungry ghost.

By night, silver moonbeams polish each turret and spire so the city shines like a pond of alabaster lilies. By day, terraces bathe, supine, in golden sunlight. Year by year, the city swirls around itself like a river of lotuses in which no one ever drowns.

For forty million years and from a hundred thousand worlds ago, precious beings have lived there, each awaiting the perfect time to awaken.

Listen, and you will hear just how it comes to pass that one among them attains the supreme enlightened state, the incomparable nirvana, exquisite teaching of formless form.

Mahāmāyā

In the same precipitous hour that spring is born, she has a vivid dream.

On a distant mountainside a pure white elephant keeps watch over her while pacing back and forth between dripping sala trees. At the sound of temple bells, the elephant steps off a ragged ledge and glides on roiling clouds toward her bedchamber. With a pure white lotus held at the tip of one of its six prodigious trunks, the elephant steps down lightly in front of Mahāmāyā. He walks three times around her high-platform, jewel-encrusted bed, and then, without sound or effort, the elephant enters through her right side, instantly concealed within her womb.

Awakening, Mahāmāyā summons her husband, King Śuddhodana, who then calls for the six royal seers to foretell a thousand true effects from this most auspicious sign.

They swarm around her body, listening at her womb, peering at her profile, until finally they agree that a son will be born distinguished by the favor of the gods. He will become the greatest of kings, the noblest leader of men! Yes, most certainly.

However, the most honored of the seers breaks away from the group and announces to the king and queen, "All that has been said is true. However, if he should ever leave the palace grounds, he will cast all privilege and love aside and become an ascetic, a holy man. But you needn't worry. Even if this happens, he will be universally adored, for he will give the people what they truly hunger for—he will become the Awakened One."

King Śuddhodana

But he does worry. In a troubling yet strangely peaceful dream, he dreams of a lotus pond so large that it has no edge, no shore of any kind. He, the king with his entourage, stands above it all, entranced and horrified at the thickened, noxious brew churning at the surface of the water.

Then his child, the one not yet even born, springs from his arms and jumps nakedly and alone into the lotus pond. The king cannot move or speak; no one can. The threefold world and thousands of gods watch as King Śuddhodana's infant son easily swims away. None of the mud sticks to his skin. He rides the current without strain, like an ivory swan. With a tranquil smile and steady gaze he looks back at his father.

Finally the king regains the power of his limbs and wit and jumps into the water after his son. But his seven-layered robes drag, and he struggles mightily. Just at the moment when he touches his son's hand he rouses from his sleep with a gasp and a sob. He looks out from his fine wide couch, awake, but unsure of where he is. His hands are shaking, still, with a residue of fear.

Mahāmāyā

On the night of a full moon, Mahāmāyā passes through the Lumbinī gardens, accompanied by pealing bells and swansongs throbbing in the evening air. Tiny rabbits hop across the pathways. She wanders further, among fragrant blossoms, until she comes to a sala tree that gently lowers one of its branches to meet her hand.

She stands very still. All sentient beings, it seems, conspire in energetic joy. She smiles. And a moment later a lovely child steps out of her side.

How the heavens tremble! The earth quivers and the oceans sigh. A pure, tranquil light appears in a broad swath across the sky.

Instantly, the sick are rid of suffering and madmen recover reason. Horses exhibit signs of excessive joy, and elephants, in solemn and resounding voice, express their gladness in deep harmonies never heard before in the history of humankind.

All sentient beings offer their adoration. Mahāmāyā can only watch in awe as he stands in a firm and upright posture upon the ground and looks out to each of the ten directions with the resolution that in every realm only he is holy; only he is sublime. "This is my last birth," he proclaims. "There shall be for me no other state of existence."

Birds of the air stand still in amazement, forgetting their usual flight; all animals give pause; rivers suspend their meandering course, seized with a mighty astonishment. Hundreds of thousands of worlds simultaneously approach each other and embrace.

At which point Siddhārtha begins to walk steadily, straight ahead. A chief of the Brahmas holds a white umbrella over his head and a wise man brings forth, for the brilliant infant, a golden fan.

Avalokiteśvara

Once called, she becomes the universal door. There is no dwindling end in the ten directions where one cannot present one's life as a plea at her gate. With her thirty-three forms and eighty-four thousand heads, she will turn to listen, and listen, and listen again. She will hear all.

If anyone should be lost at sea and call on Avalokiteśvara, he or she will find a shallow place. Even if hundreds, thousands, and millions of living beings flounder in the great ocean, if one of them calls on her true name, they will, each one of them, become free at once and safe to journey forward. She is the thousand-handed and thousand-eyed. Once called, she becomes the most intimate, eternal companion.

Therefore, when King Śuddhodana asks that the infant Siddhārtha be given over to her care, Avalokiteśvara answers with the cosmos at her beck and call. She takes the name of nursemaid. She answers with her entire being. With perfect joy, Avalokiteśvara postpones ascending to the heavenly realm so that she might protect him.

Rabbit

A young rabbit cannot help but spring, leap, or vault over whatever happens to appear in front of him. The twig in the grass, a cricket. An outcrop of rock. It's all one to him, all a universe of energetic joy that he is destined and determined to attain.

BOSTON

Massachusetts, US, 21st c. CE

She is an elder sister of New England, long-suffering, high-minded, and perhaps a little hard of hearing. Nevertheless she will stay and hold court until the bitter end. Underneath her ponderous redbrick skirts, cars dodge and squeal. While far above, at her square shoulders, Boston fragments the sky with sheer facades of echoing light. She is a fortress that holds her convictions firm—all of her fifty-two colleges and universities concur—perseverance overcomes every ill.

After blizzards, precious tons of salt are spread on the city streets. And in a heavy wind she feeds her citizens on blown-out shards of glass, or slivers of gin, whichever comes first.

Her citizens make the best of things and their children grow up strong enough, or otherwise as best they can.

The houses, oh the houses, how they endure even as they rot away! Along the major avenues, trees display a grandmotherly green demeanor. The asphalt winks at bookish pedestrians in the rain. The city waits patiently, no matter how long it takes, for that singular citizen who will come out of it all unscathed.

Maya

In the dream, she reaches in her belly and cradles the heel of her child's foot. Then her hand, with the whole fetus cupped within, floats as a piece of driftwood lapping up against a calm, wide shore. Her unborn child jumps out and sets down an anchor in the sand.

The sky is too bright. He will burn, and already there's nothing she can do. Try as she might to be practical, she can only watch from behind a distant cloud. He is impossibly thin and inconceivably strong.

She's never felt, until this moment, such extremes of love and loss. Now, as she awakens, she knows that as soon as her son is born to her, he will never again belong to her, not to her body or even her mind.

Then she wakes, feeling for a glass of water in the predawn darkness.

Nearly three months later, Maya's driving back from the grocery store, listening to her Doc Watson playlist, when she suddenly has to pull off the road to vomit over a white picket fence. Weakened, shaking, she returns to the car and realizes that she will, forever more, turn green at the sound of his voice—the old passion for country music and slide guitar suddenly dead in water, never to be reborn.

The implications are clear. Anyone can love good music

and white picket fences till the cows come home, but cause and effect are a potent brew. Just do the dry math, she tells herself. Nothing to cry about here. If one cause (pregnancy) has ten thousand effects (the association of Doc Watson with morning sickness being just one) and each effect gives birth (so to speak) to a new cause, what, in sum total, will she have given birth to?

Sid

In the first moment he curls into himself, as if contained still. The universe that was his mother's womb now spreads, alarmingly, in all directions. At once he means to test its limit. When he pushes out a knee and stretches out a hand, magically, a blanket of cool air plays against his skin. Then opening his eyes, he squints, trying too hard to see what is right in front of his nose. So bright, almost too brilliant to bear—still, he takes easily to this new universe and claims it as his natural birthright, his very own dominion and home.

Maya

Look at you—such a pale, astonished being, stricken by my missing warmth—don't look back at me. Rather, be thrilled in ten different ways by the kaleidoscopic reflections of your very first breath. I don't mean to be so nakedly in love, but it's your only inheritance and it's true.

Because of me and ten thousand other causes, you've materialized, spilled out of a cesarean section gone wrong. Confused and woefully ill equipped, you will have to take up the gauntlet of cause and effect on your own now, Sid. And good luck with that. Shine a light on it, little one. I'm already running out of blood and breath and time and have to keep these very last thoughts real, for you.

Ava

We midwives roll the dice, and we do what we know or don't know how to do. It can be a sorry business sometimes, that's for sure. I'm telling you straight, we try with all we've got. If we stood any closer we'd be taking the mother's place ourselves. What else can I say? Sometimes mothers still die.

But you made it out okay, Sid. Welcome to our little show-stopping, precious life. It's a revolving debut, like the doors in front of Macy's. Welcome to our hocus-pocus brave new world, kiddo. I'm telling you—every time a new child appears, it's another miracle.

Word of advice: look quick, look sharp; look up and down and in all directions before life moves on without you. Because I know for a fact that in a minute the world will turn its attention elsewhere—to midtown traffic, stock market tallies, or truck-loads of data-entry love notes dumped in the city drains, and who knows what else.

Astonishing, isn't it, Sid? Look close, sweet nothing child— it's a rude shock, a routine slap meant to make you breathe yourself alive.

YOUTH

Siddhārtha

The beloved spring festival begins—a grand procession of a thousand ploughs and a thousand pairs of oxen garlanded in flame-colored flowers. All the noblemen follow after, dressed in their silver finery. They play and pretend to be plowing fields, and included among them is the king, in gold. Fools prance around the spectators pulling frogs and rabbits from hats and setting them free at the feet of pretty young maidens.

Infant Siddhārtha lays content in the shade of a nearby jambu tree. His attendant nurses, distracted by the joyful clamor, wander from his side.

Seeing no one close by, Siddhārtha sits up, folds his legs crosswise, and absorbs himself in serene meditation, though he is only three months old. Without thought, body, or mind, breathing in and out, breath merges with a passing golden wind, and he smiles.

Avalokiteśvāra

For the first three years of Siddhārtha's life, she has watched as everyone who meets him brings gifts: tiny animals, deer and elephants, horses, cows, birds, and fish. All are made of precious and rare materials, decorated with gems that outweigh his body threefold times.

Patiently, she stands by as each morning Siddhārtha is dressed in the finest silks. His servants play with him by decorating his long, thin arms and legs and neck. Earrings hang heavily from his ears, drawing down his lobes to his shoulders. He stands patiently and submits to their whims. If others laugh, he laughs. It is all one to him.

But finally Avalokiteśvara strides into Siddhārtha's bedroom where he sits adorned in jewelry and she admonishes the servants. "If the earth were made of gold, a single ray of light from this child, the world's future guide, would be enough to dull its splendor. The light of the stars and the light of the moon, even the light of the sun, are dimmed by his natural brilliance.

"Why then would you have him wear jewels, baubles crudely fashioned by mere jewelers and goldsmiths? Remove these trifles. Give them away. This child will have his thoughts; they are gems of a purer water."

King Śuddhodana

Ruler of the Śākya race, celebrated as the brightest ornament of the realm—who can match his splendor? Without effort honors come easily to his hand. His manner, all his life, has been kindly and just. As he pursues his bravest enemies, they fall before him as readily as elephants are overcome by the heat of the sun. As he hunts in the forest, tigers wait patiently for his arrow. Most intimately he is beloved of his many consorts.

Why then, with all the glory and pleasures thus accrued, does he pine so persistently for the one that has gone?

It is as if his wife, Mahāmāyā, had merely strayed into the world, just long enough to come of age and then leave behind the torment of her beauty on the face of their beloved son. The earth knew her only briefly; whereupon she was returned to the sky gods, a gift half given and then entirely taken away.

A mockery, an inexplicable fate, that she should have given their child the name Siddhārtha, meaning "wish fulfilled." Whose wish? Even though he, the supreme and powerful King Śuddhodana, cannot attain the promise of such a name, he will do all in his power to see that his son can. Everything from his slightest to boldest desire will be provided. And Siddhārtha will never be so heartlessly taken away from his side. It will not be allowed.

Siddhārtha

Thus he grows in accomplishments and beauty, as easily as sunlight climbs from the eastern mountains and as rapidly as fire fanned by auspicious winds. Three palaces are given him, one for each season of the year. Each nine stories high and filled with jewels and childlike entertainments, his royal dwellings tower among the common huts so that he never has to set foot on the ordinary anguish of this world.

His father, diligent in his love, spares no expense to insure that his delicate son will have all that he wishes. Wherever Siddhārtha places his head, a white parasol appears above it so that a perfect weather will always be sustained.

But every perfection pales against the child's curiosity—whenever a speck of dust is swept away, he longs to explore its origins all the way back to the forbidden, and therefore fascinating, muddy ground.

One day he sneaks out of the palace at dawn. Having caught a whiff of unfamiliar things, he pursues the scent: something moist and dense, tangled in flavors of earthy brown. Wandering, he comes to an immeasurable field. There he sees a peasant, sickened by the heat, whipping a unwilling ox to pull a heavy plow. They strain and drag themselves up and down, carving furrows in the earth to plant seeds. Overturned soil exposes a mass of worms, beetles, and centipedes writhing in distress.

Siddhārtha, riveted to the scene, then realizes why so many small excited birds hover nearby. Chattering with joy, they feast on the frantic bugs. Just then, a hawk swoops down, catches one of the birds in its claws, and takes to the air giving out a loud victorious call.

Siddhārtha cries out and instantly his father appears out of nowhere, swoops him up in his arms, and says, "What are you doing here? This is not your play pavilion, nor your sanctioned imperial view."

Out from under his father's arm, Siddhārtha catches a final glimpse. The plowman stumbles, then regains his footing. Siddhārtha rubs his ankle, and feels the place where pain swells. And then he can hardly breathe, as if he were not in his father's arms at all, but grasped in the hawk's talons, carried high above, with only this single moment left to live.

Hawk

A beef would describe it well, as that is what we fight over in the middle of the field—small delectable birds! Tail feathers bruised and tangled! Oh my, but it does get the heart pounding away! All this undignified, madcap scuffle and grab just to stay gloriously alive.

Sid

Dust motes sail across the nursery room on an invisible current of shifting light. How glorious it is! Sid awakens in wondrous equanimity, with all the baby monitors in the house tuned in to his slightest move.

Among the many teddy bears scattered in the crib, he manages to sit upright, then wavers a bit before centering his spine.

"Well done, mazel tov." Ava, his nanny, whispers, "Hold steady, kiddo."

Heavy-headed, Sid shifts his gaze and catches sight of his ten different toes, each more absorbing than the last, each an independent miracle. What is this? And this? And this? His center of gravity leans first to those toes and then to a rudimentary turn of thought—is he performer or audience?

A moment later he decides to forego the question (an intriguing development).

But then, in an amateur's ploy for kisses, he reaches out to Ava. Ah, the fate of those dimpled legs folded on their briefest of laurels! Of course he misses his target and falls on his side. Even as he wails bitterly, even as she kisses him gently and sets him upright again, she says, "Sid, just try again. Even if you fall down seven times, get over it and get up again for eight."

Ava

Ava washes the dishes, even though it's not written up in her job description. It's been six years that she's been looking after the professor and his son. Even though the professor scatters his half-finished coffee cups on every horizontal surface in the house, even though she has ten other things to do before she can take a break and get back to her current ten-thousand-piece puzzle, she's used to doing what needs doing. A magician, she's not. She just likes to get things done. Why should she catalog her chores in some arbitrary ledger of give and take, good and bad, fair or unfair? She takes great satisfaction in making use of her eyes, her hands, her mind. Then her tiny, bone-tired body sometimes transforms into something light and joyous. Sure, it's a mystery and wonder, how that happens. In other words, it's a fine day; she has no complaints.

Ava dries her hands and then walks down the hallway to check on Sid. Her fuzzy blue slippers set off static sparks. His door swings open. A cool breeze sighs as she whispers, *Good night, sweet dreams*. She tiptoes in and kisses the boy's forehead as he turns in sleep.

After, she brings a cup to the stove and pours tea, her home-made chai with raw honey—the hotter, the better. Then she sits at the kitchen table and holds the cup by the rim, *ahhh*. She drinks, and gazes fondly at all her scattered puzzle pieces. This will be a new one, the most challenging yet, largely because most of the picture is a clear blue sky above a variably shaded blue sea. Only in the lower left-hand corner is there a high-contrast image. This, of course, is where she'll start; it is a boy bravely sailing out to great wide sea in a little pea-green boat.

Sid

He only pretends to sleep as Ava kisses him. How could he possibly fall asleep when he's been sent to bed so early, as a remedy for a single sneeze? His eyes will not close. It is a crime against childhood to be kept so much indoors. Though he actually likes to be alone, preferring his own imaginary games to the rougher play of other boys, how could he possibly go to sleep at eight o'clock?

Now Ava's closed the door. He can hear her shuffle to the kitchen. Now's his chance. If any sort of adventures are to be had, he must invent them whole cloth. Cloth, indeed!

He imagines—actually, he decides!—that he is lost at sea and he will sail across his blanket, which he instantly transforms into colossal waves. His bony knees churn beneath the underbelly of this cottony sea. He whispers a blustery wind, a slashing rain ,and a soft-whistled seagull's cry. Oh, he's in it now!

With long, thin fingers he charts a solitary course. As if lit from within, his fingertips trace the fabric's blue swirly print all the way back to an entirely different kind of shore. No knock-kneed, tongue-tied boy here. He is the bravest of ferrymen, plying the bow straight through hazardous peaks and troughs.

He is, and will forever be, loath to fall asleep. He would rather sail the uncharted universe than be treated like a child. He would prefer to plumb every depth of the unknown and come back bruised and battered than be imprisoned by a long dull night of ordinary dreams.

The next morning, Sid climbs out his bedroom window into the early morning dew. He hardly knows why. Restless, rebellious, curious—what does it matter? Ava says that he lives too much in his head. So he'll use his arms and legs! As he walks through the damp grass in his bare feet and feels the wind at his face, he almost turns back. But the cold pinching at his cheeks inspires him. He will stand sentry at the gate of spring. He will guard the crocuses in the lawn, helpless victims of last night's storm.

He imagines that he has miraculous, super-charged, bionic eyes. He will save the blighted flowers by staring at them with his instantaneous, life-enhancing powers. First one, then another, and another. Ava says that spring is too brief a season and because he loves her, he tries to raise up the yellows and purples from the grass with his laser-sharp gaze.

Even though the wind on its rampage has already shattered the blooms, and even though his approach is seriously flawed, Sid remains undeterred. Is he not the first and only son of the greatest Harvard professor of dead languages? From this day on, he decides, he will no longer be a fearful, shy, and quiet boy. He will summon up his own enormous strength and it will be worthy of any invisible wind. Aren't these scrawny limbs of his the beginnings of greater things to come?

But after a few minutes, he climbs back into his bedroom. It's freezing out there! He fumbles out of his wet pajamas, dives under the covers stark naked, and shivers himself into a feverish sleep, his dreams full of flowers falling into a great fire, each one crashing with the weight of giants.

Avalokiteśvara

While they dream fitfully, she tells both Sid and Siddhārtha this story, whispering to them from inside their hearts so that they might dream themselves as the hero of the tale, the selfless hare. Many lives ago, she says, you were reborn as a hare. You lived in a leafy forest at the edge of a grassy field surrounded by climbing vines and sweet wild orchids. Your three best friends, monkey, jackal, and otter, looked upon you, the hare, as their wise leader.

As the boys' eyelids flutter, she explains, *Yes, dear ones, the best leaders don't have to shout loud or even look big or imposing; that's their secret.*

You, the hare, taught your friends the importance of doing the right thing, in every circumstance, at any point in time. "What is the right thing?" *they asked.* "Always and everywhere," *you told them,* "be willing and ready to give. Give, and give and give, until your very last breath—that is the most important thing in life!" *You admonished your friends that if someone asked them for food, they were to give freely and generously from the food they had gathered for themselves.*

Then Avalokiteśvara stirs the dream into lifelike proportions. No longer speaking words, she wills the boys to live the dream by themselves.

Śakra, lord of devas, watches the four friends, hare, monkey, jackal, and otter, from his great palace of marble and light on the peak of Mount Meru. He decides to test their compassion and resolve.

Just then the four friends disperse to find food for the day. The otter discovers seven red fish floundering on a riverbank; the jackal finds a lizard and a vessel of curdled milk someone had abandoned; the monkey gathers mangoes from the trees.

Śakra takes the form of a priest, and he goes to the otter and says, "Friend, I am hungry. Can you help me?" And the otter offers the seven fish he had gathered for his own meal.

Then Śakra goes to the jackal, and says, "Friend, I am hungry. I need food before I can perform my priestly duties. Can you help me?" And the jackal offers the priest the lizard and curdled milk he had planned to have for his own meal.

Then Śakra goes to the monkey, and says, "Friend, I am hungry. Can you help me?" And the monkey offers the juicy mangoes he had so looked forward to eating himself.

Then Śakra goes to the hare and asks for food, but the hare has no food other than the grass growing in the forest, a diet that a man could not eat. So the hare tells the priest to build a fire, and when the fire is burning strongly, he says, "I have nothing to give you to eat but myself!" Then the hare throws himself into the fire.

Śakra, still disguised as a priest, is astonished and deeply moved. He causes the fire to be cold so the hare is not burned. Then he reveals his true form to the selfless little hare. "Dear hare," he says, "your virtue will be remembered through the ages." Whereupon Śakra paints the wise hare's likeness on the pale face of the moon, for all to see and admire.

Śakra returns to his home on Mount Meru, and the four friends live long and happily in their beautiful forest. And to this day, those who look up at the moon can see the image of the selfless hare gazing fondly back at them.

Hare

Please do not distract yourselves with the irrelevant argument about what you see. Is it a hare or a man in the moon? Who cares! As for me, I am only grinding the elixir of life into golden dust between my jaws, letting the dust scatter at your feet.

Siddhārtha

Across the broad sapphire sky, a flock of white swans fly north to the quiet estuaries of the Himalayan foothills. Devadatta, cousin to the prince, aims his bow and finds his target in the wing of the whitest, most majestic swan. As it falls fast to the earth, Siddhārtha races to the injured bird and gently takes it in his lap. He sits with knees crossed, soothing the wild thing even as its red garnet blood seeps into the ground. With light, kind palms as soft as plantain leaves he composes its ruffled feathers and calms its racing heart. With his left hand he holds the bird close and with his right he draws out the arrow.

Though he knows little of the bird's pain he cries for its sting, and with tears he soothes his bird and says to all that surround them, "Now you are mine, and I will care for you."

But Devadatta answers, "The wild thing belongs to the one who fetched it down."

Siddhārtha lays the swan's neck beside his own smooth cheek saying, "No, the bird is mine."

Many couriers and nobles reason and argue back and forth, until an unknown priest arises among them and says, "If life is precious, then the savior of a life owns the responsibility for the living thing; more so than the one who sought to slay it. The slayer spoils and wastes, the cherisher sustains; therefore give Siddhārtha the bird, temporarily. When the bird can fly again, it will belong to no one other than the clear blue sky."

All find this wise judgment just, but when the king turns to honor the sage he has disappeared. Someone sees a hooded snake glide away. The many people gathered there whisper among themselves that the gods often come and go in this way. Like life, or like death, or like clouds in a summer's rain.

King Śuddhodana

The king watches from the back of the royal classroom, meaning merely to observe his son's progress with numbers. The royal numerologist says, "Repeat after me, Siddhārtha. Together, we will recite your numerations until we reach the lakh—one, two, three, four, to ten, and then by tens to hundreds and thousands."

After him, Siddhārtha steadily names digits, then decades, centuries. Nor does he pause on reaching the round lakh, but easily he continues on his own, "Then comes the koti, nahut, ninnahut, and on to the pundarikas and padumas, the last of which is how you count the grains of Kapilavastu if it were to be ground to finest dust. Beyond that there is a numeration called the katha, used to count the stars at night; then the koti-katha, for the ocean drops; ingga, for the calculus of circles, till we come to the four types of kalpas culminating in maha-kalpas, the greatest unit of time. By these means of computing, the gods resolve the future and the past.'"

"'Tis good," the sage replies briskly, "'tis good." Though to King Śuddhodana's eye, the numerologist looks terrified, as he quickly bundles up his notes and books, bowing deeply before Siddhārtha, again and again, backing away into interior rooms.

The king himself is baffled and amazed. He's heard of kalpas—who has not?—but he cannot really grasp the concept himself and so he asks Siddhārtha, bowing in his great bulk of garments and jewels to his son, "How long is a maha-kalpa?"

"Father, imagine a colossal mountain at the beginning of a kalpa, approximately sixteen miles high. If a bird were to take a small piece of silk in its beak and wipe the mountain once every hundred years, the mountain will be completely worn away even before the kalpa ends."

"Dearest son, how many kalpas have come before this one?"

Siddhārtha replies, "If you count the total number of sand particles at the depths of the Ganges river, from where it begins to where it ends at the sea, even that number will be less than the number of passed kalpas."

"Truly, that is the most remarkable fact that I have ever heard!"

But Siddhārtha looks out the window, his brow furrowed.

"What is it, son? What disturbs your heart, when you have so much brilliance, both within and without?"

"It is the question 'why' that confounds me, Father, not 'how many.' Why do time and space exist? Why do we live? Why am I overcome with passions? Why do I tremble with fear in the night?"

Rat

Time and space cannot be seen, but I trust they begin here,
at this flimsy, swaying thread strung between two unknowns.
Wind quivers through my whiskers. Hope permeates the view,
and just as I question the wisdom of this next step, I take to my
high-wire act and run.

Sudovsky

Professor Sudovsky waits at the entrance to Boylston Hall for his son and his son's nanny. He's to spend quality time with the boy. He's been advised by his son's school counselor in a singularly unsavory manner, as if he, the father, were to blame. As if his son's "accidents"—what an evasive word!—as if his son's inability to remember to go to the bathroom was the fault of a single father who does what he bloody well can to take care of his endless obligations. The accidents happen because the boy is brilliant. His mind is preoccupied with precocious original thoughts.

Therefore it is only natural that he, the father, now cast as adversary, feels somewhat ambivalent if not resentful of the assignment. Quality time! What a trivialized, foolish term. Of course he loves his son and of course he would do anything for him. How dare they imply otherwise.

Professor Sudovsky fights with his jacket's buttons and

their buttonholes. For what the garment cost, it could function more freely. He glares at the expanse of Harvard Yard and its procession of earnest youth crisscrossing the green. Professor Sudovsky should be going over his PhD candidates' theses. He should be writing his article for *The Indo-European Linguistic Scholars Review*.

At the parent-teacher conferences last week, Sid's barely literate school counselor began with the usual accolades—*He's a bright boy, but—*. Of course he's a bright boy! As if any offspring of theirs could possibly be otherwise. Professor Sudovsky feels the familiar stab of pain. Maya had been the better one, with better mental acuity and brighter wit—a wiser, kinder human being.

He snips off, no, he strangulates that line of feeling. It will not bleed out of him further. How readily it seeps, even after these interminable six years without her.

Ah, there they are. Sid, being the shy boy that he is, walks just behind Ava, clinging to her sweater's sleeve. Ava, he sees, has to place the boy's hand in his own. He takes it, and instantly, as always happens, a tear springs to his eye and he must fight it off even as he grasps the child's thin hot hand firmly. "Sid. Good boy. Good day today," he says, looking up at Ava uncertainly, but Ava, it seems, has already gone, as if evaporated in thin air.

Professor Sudovsky looks down at his boy and asks, "Shall we go to the donut shop in Harvard Square? Would you like that?"

The boy nods and smiles. Professor Sudovsky nods too and smiles broadly. What a beautiful boy. "Ah, yes, yes, okay then. Am I to assume that it will be a Boston Creme? Would that be one, or two?"

Sid

Sid knows he's chattering away like a magpie at a Mardi Gras parade, that's what Ava calls his storytelling, but he can hardly stop himself. He's stored up so much to tell! First and foremost is the plan that he's worked out on how to travel from star to star. With a set of springs in his shoes, he's convinced it can be attained. But then he wants to explain about magpies. "Dad, did you know that magpies are one of the few kinds of animals that can recognize themselves in the mirror? Did you know that magpies are related to crows, which happen to be incredibly smart, kind of like Ivy-leaguers among birds?"

Then Sid stops cold, transfixed, in the middle of the street. His eyes simultaneously shy away and stare as his heart holds still. What he sees there is too hard to fathom. A flattened rabbit: fresh roadkill. And perched avidly on that beautiful, soft, and bloodied fur, a crow pecks at the rabbit's insides.

Sid shivers, and feels the crow devouring the rabbit's guts, and also, shifting, feels the rabbit still dying, his own child's body turning sticky wet, and cold.

Sudovsky

He sees the problem: it is already too late to shield his son from the gruesome sight. Parenting is an impossible responsibility, and yet there is no alternative. To fend off his son's pain, he takes up the only weapon he knows, the default setting hard-wired into his brain: language. And wanting to heal his child—wounded as he must be by this perfunctory sight of death—Professor Sudovsky tries to distract, pulling him away from the rabbit and the crow, all the while speaking of facts, like performing a slight-of-hand, anything to make a dead rabbit disappear.

"Sid, did you know that the word *corpse*, meaning dead body, comes from the Latin *corpus*? However, the word in Pali is *chava*. An interesting linguistic tic—though it's spelled with a *ch*, it's still a sibilant. Do you know what sibilant means, Sid? No? You can look it up in the dictionary when we get home."

Sid

Later that afternoon, Sid searches back and forth through gossamer-thin pages. *Sibilant*—a most slippery word. He asks, "Does it begin with an *s* or *c*?" Of course, he's asking this question in the high, squeaky voice that annoys his father no end. But how can he help it if he's not yet a professor at the age of six? Really!

"Look it up," his father says. "Find truth and meaning for yourself. That's what the dictionary is there for—a beautiful thing." Professor Sudovsky stands to one side and strokes the massive stack of words. "Nothing distinguishes between the powerful and meek as much as knowledge, Sid. Every page of this dictionary opens up more riches."

Riches don't happen to interest Sid, and what a burden these words can turn out to be! He frowns and eyes his father sideways, knowing well enough not to ask for any more clues. Bitterly, he decides that *sibilant* must begin with *c*, followed by an *i*. Sid's legs tire. His eyes itch. Clearly his young life is defined by suffering. He wonders if death is the absence of pain. Could he achieve a point in between and thereby escape both? He buries himself in the dictionary's spine. He pours his whole heart into doing as his father asked. Though the task is too much for even a precociously intelligent little boy, Sid scans word after word. Even with perfect eyesight, how should he search for something that has no discernible characteristics?

C, then *i*, and then must come a *b*…. Pouring sound over symbol, *sibilant* is a cruel word; it hisses like a snake that eats dictionaries and little boys for breakfast. He shudders, remembering the dead rabbit. He recalls its dull eyes staring into space. Sid whimpers, "Actually, my eyes—"

"No excuses, son. To search is already to find."

Sid starts to cry. "Then what is it that I've found so far? What?"

Ava

Ava sits with Sid on his bed, his head cradled in her arms. The poor boy spent the entire hour before dinner searching for that miserable word, until finally the professor gave in and helped the boy. Poor kid. If that whole production was meant to distract him from the spectacle of life and death on the street, she sincerely doubts its worth. Ava pinches Sid's cheek lovingly.

"How about I tell you a funny story that doesn't have any words in it, Sid? Or at least not very many. I do have to begin, after all, with *Once upon a time…*"

Sid nods and hiccups as a few last tears roll down his face.

"Once upon a time it was said, 'Two's company and three's a crowd,' but what about four and five?"

"Oh, Ava, you can't fool me so easily! Four and five equals nine." And he giggles.

Good. Maybe now she can work a little lightness into his overeducated mind. "Okay, here's another one. What did the zero say to the eight?"

Sid tenses in her lap, clenches his little fists. She lets a moment pass. Oh, she's wicked…better help him out before the waterworks start up again. "Want me to tell you?"

Sid nods. She knows how he hates not knowing things. Better get used to it, kiddo! She waits, then smiles so wide that he can't help himself, and smiles too. "Still want me to tell you?"

"Yes!"

"What did the zero say to the eight? He said, 'Nice belt you have on there!'"

Sid slides off her lap onto the floor, laughing so hard he starts to cry again, this time from sheer foolishness and joy. Finally!

Maya

She watches from every vantage point of the cosmos as Sid tiptoes down the hall with his offering for today. He tapes a new drawing to the TV, believing she lives just behind the monitor, so Maya leans in to admire his handiwork.

Part rabbit, part crow, and something akin to a little boy—the sketch is figured with sturdy rabbit's feet, feathers brushed on in all directions, and a bright compassion in its childlike eyes that only a dead mother could have recognized.

Sid sits cross-legged in front of the TV, back straight and ears aligned to his young shoulders. He waits, unwavering, for Maya to appear so that he can ask her to explain death to him. He is a stubborn boy. She tells him this in the form of an ache between his shoulder blades and a twitch in his left eye.

He is also a kind boy, with an unguarded, open heart capable of hearing the anguish of others. And after a time, she tells him this too—in the guise of a warm stillness filling up the space at his center with her widest smile.

Crow

With feet planted firmly in the intestines, I find delight in my life. Regrettably it is a partial repast. Knowing I'll be elbowed out by bigger brutes, I will have to eat quite fast. And with every swallow, know I'll be hungry again and never quite get my due.

Rabbit

When I had eyes I remembered a certain light green leaf trembling. And on my tongue, a fear stirred—like a strand of reddish blue drawn from a pool of dark reflections yet to occur. So faint it was that I dared not move. Or breathe, or live again.

LOVE & FAMILY LIFE

Siddhārtha

Silvery curtains of rain sway outside the palace walls, therefore Siddhārtha stays inside from morning to night. On first opening his eyes at dawn, a musician plays a warbler's song on a golden flute and three dancing girls attend to his needs in a cloud of silks and shawls. On closing his eyes at night, a procession of acrobats and poets accompany him to his bed.

He never thinks of leaving. His limbs tire even before they move. Therefore he is carried. As one who is drugged in Brahmanic ritual, he ascends and descends the stairs in a fog of entertainments.

As the years go by even the natural world bends to his slightest needs. One day, he sits under the jambu tree on a summer afternoon, idling away the hours, but the shade, rather than following the sun's path, stays locked in place above him, to protect the divine young man from any harmful rays.

Siddhārtha listens to a magpie cry in the distant forest and recalls a deep disquiet, something he witnessed, by chance, as a young child. He resolves to see again the natural world and he sets his heart on an expedition, far away from palace enchantments.

When the king hears of it, he orders slaves to precede his son and clear away all afflictions from the path. Once the road is sufficiently strewn with blossoms, incense, and glittering coins, the prince's golden chariot takes leave. Like the moon mounting to the sky, he proceeds with a suitable retinue.

Peasants crowd at the roadside to catch sight of him. From nearby windows, faces of glorious women with their earrings resting on each other's cheeks appear like bouquets of lotus flowers.

When the prince asks his charioteer to stop, he sees, in their midst, a woman with strange white hair. Her limbs are twisted and discolored. He watches, horrified, as she sinks to the ground with her hand, riddled in a maze of lines, stretching out to him.

"What is this?" he asks his driver. "Is this some transformation in her, or her original state, or mere chance?"

"It is old age," the charioteer admits, "that which has broken her down, the murderer of beauty and the ruin of good health. She is a woman that has grown old and soon will die."

King Śuddhodana

King Śuddhodana looks on his son as he wanders the palace grounds in a sleepwalker's stupor, under a cloud of melancholy. Dark shadows loom under Siddhārtha's eyes and a hundred bright melodies orchestrated from the courtyards cannot dispel them. If permitted, Siddhārtha would sleep twenty hours in the space of twenty-four. Ever since the boy crossed paths with the woman overtaken by old age, he has lived as one haunted by suffering.

Measures must be taken. King Śuddhodana makes an announcement to the entire region. In seven days' time, Siddhārtha will present gifts to the young women of the city. To Siddhārtha, he says, "I only ask that you pick one, and she will be your queen from whom your seed will bring out a dozen sons. The beautiful women, all five hundred of them, are insensible to wines, as meek as slaves. Siddhārtha, pick a wife and live close by her unblemished side. Stay at home, with us, and never leave."

Siddhārtha

The next day, the young women arrive to the great hall of the palace and the room is filled with their extravagant beauty displayed in flowing silks and blossoms. In ceremonial order, each woman is presented to him, and to each one, Siddhārtha presents a jewel. But Siddhārtha sees none distinctly and barely moves beyond handing them their token gifts.

Yasodharā is the last one to appear before him. She advances fearlessly, without even blinking her eyes. But by this time, Siddhārtha hasn't a single jewel left. Yasodharā smiles and says, "Prince, in what way have I offended you?"

"You have not offended me," he replies, at once startled into paying attention to this bold, inscrutable woman. He looks up and recognizes her as the daughter of his father's close friend, Daṇḍapāṇi. Siddhārtha has known her all his life. But now, as if for the first time, he see her as the grown woman she is, with magnificent grace and beauty. Gently, he replies, "I mean no offense. It is just that you are the last one and I have no jewel left to give you."

But then he remembers that on his finger he is wearing a ring of great value that had been given him from his mother, inherited from her grandmother. He takes it off and hands it to Yasodharā.

Yasodharā, however, does not take it, and says, "Prince, must I accept this ring from you?"

"It was mine and you must accept it."

"No," she says, "I will not deprive you of your jewels. It is for me, rather, to give you a jewel."

Then she walked away, trailing a long and mystifying scent after her.

No more than a week after this meeting, Siddhārtha strives to win her hand. To appease Yasodharā's father, he must prove himself adept at more than wealth and social standing. Therefore a competition among all the young men of the kingdom is proclaimed. The competitors align themselves along the palace wall, each with his own bow and arrow, each with his own ambitions, talents, and dreams.

Skillful archers send their arrows into targets that are barely discernible to the naked eye.

But when it is the prince's turn to shoot, so great is his natural strength that he breaks each bow as he draws it out. Finally, the king sends guards to fetch an ancient, precious bow that has been stored within the temple treasury. No one within the memory of humankind has ever been able to draw or lift it.

Siddhārtha takes the bow in his left hand, and with one finger of his right hand he draws it to himself. Then he takes as target a tree so far away that he alone can see it. The arrow pierces straight through the tree and buries itself in the ground beyond, utterly disappeared. And there, where the arrow has entered the ground, a well of pure, fresh water spontaneously bubbles forth.

Siddhārtha and Yasodharā

Soon thereafter, the two marry and their joy creates days, months, and years of perfect weather and bountiful pleasure for all that are blessed to live nearby. Daily the two lovers celebrate each other by word and touch, shifting the site of their passion between their three palaces.

Cool marble fountains, refreshing pools in the midst of gardens—all seamlessly accompany the tenderly entwined bodies of Siddhārtha and Yasodharā. Strolling up and down the stairs, musicians improvise to the tune of their ecstatic cries.

Prince Siddhārtha never says anything that is not beautiful to Yasodharā's ears, nor does he see any aspect of his beloved that is not sweet and pleasant to his eyes.

They roll off a rooftop on which they are making love and fall, landing in a bed of lotuses and lilies, not even noticing they have fallen.

King Śuddhodana

The king's love for his son now verges on abject adoration. Infinite care is taken to direct Siddhārtha's views. Śuddhodana builds balustrades for where his son might wish to climb and balconies for where he might wish to gaze outside. Each plank and column of wood is examined by Śuddhodana's own hand for slivers or abrasive edge.

While Śuddhodana's hands grow coarse, the delicate prince drains his cup of pleasure to the dregs. At every event, the king commands an uplifting mood for Siddhārtha and his young wife. When the silver, jewel-encrusted bell is struck, jovial acrobats appear and perform to the sound of golden kettledrums. Their games amuse. Laughter flits between the rooms like butterflies.

Yet Śuddhodana judges himself with the utmost severity. He must keep his soul serene and refrain from doing harm. As wild horses are made to bear the yoke, so does he subdue his passions. He never utters a word that is pleasant and yet a lie; the truths told never give offense. He tries, with the wide, all-encompassing effort of a water god, to be just.

And still Śuddhodana and the citizens of the kingdom seem to be holding their breath, asking without uttering the words, *How long will it last?*

For a full seven years Kapilavastu is the happiest of cities. And yet whenever Śuddhodana smiles, a tear hangs at the corner of his eye. He knows, like he knows the name of every citizen of the kingdom, that Siddhārtha has always been a most curious, compassionate son. The time for change ripens. Soon a change will come and he will lose what, in reality, never belonged to him in the first place.

Rabbit

Disembodied merchandise. Grasping fur around a severed joint, I am my own black-and-white enigma. My own foot. These translucent claws. Without me, without even memory.

From where, then, does this voice come? A dream? The question itself has claws and digs deep into some other, unimaginable skin.

Sid

His best friends, Lane and Monty, slouch, sipping bubble tea to go. Sid imitates the way Lane walks and the way he hunches his shoulders with his chin caved in. Together they cultivate an aimless pace, with the unspoken destination of the Charles River by way of the Astrology Club for Girls, which is a bit of a detour but worth it.

Sid feels for his lucky rabbit's foot, tucked deep in his pocket. He blushes against the chance he'll run into Yasmin, the daughter of one of his father's friends at Harvard. Lane and Monty know it. Everybody knows it. What it is alternately terrifies and draws him on like a magnetic force. However, at just this moment, he'd rather run the other way.

Sid says, "I don't think the rowers will be out today. It's too hot."

Of course as soon as he opens his mouth he knows he's pathetically obvious. But it's too late now.

Lane mock-wails. Monty laughs. Sid blushes some more.

"Your boat to sink," Monty says. "Personally, I'd like to break into the boathouse and take a few kayaks out on the river. Anyone game?"

Everyone's not saying anything. Finally Monty comes up with another plan. "Movies?"

It's what they end up doing every Saturday afternoon. Even their free days become another invitation to slide into the torpor of routine. Anything to avoid the sheer terror of the unknown.

Ava

She watches Sid toss pebbles across the green. She knows he meant for them to land in the pond with a singular, eye-catching splash. But instead, the pebbles drop silently in the grass just a little shy of water. Look at the boy—with hands and feet too large and mismatched for his narrow frame. And how spectacularly unathletic he is!

He believes he's too old to be accompanied by his nanny to the Boston Public Garden and he tries to keep his distance. Ava sympathizes, and to a point she agrees with the boy. But the professor believes thieves and hooligans lie in wait, just for Sid. Sooner or later the boy will have to go out into the world on his own.

Sid kicks at the grass and halftrips over his own feet. Ava smiles. The unflagging love, there it is again. Poor boy. He should take up sports, build up some muscle!

She calls to him, "Sid, have you thought of trying out for junior crew next year? I hear they hire local boys to pedal the swan boats. It'd be a great workout for you this summer."

She turns, distracted by a handsome man passing by, a

Houdini making off with a piece of her heart in the back pocket of his jeans. She sighs. In another life, another time.

Sid doesn't answer but calls back with a question of his own. "When will anything ever take flight, soar, or blast off?"

She wants to say, If you looked about you, you'd see sparrows, butterflies, hearts, pebbles, crows, time, airplanes, all sorts of flying things... but she doesn't. Silence, sometimes, is a more astute instructor. Instead, she looks after her Houdini as he disappears behind the hot dog stand.

Meanwhile, black midges fly above their heads. She watches Sid as he swats at one. Then he looks at his hands, quietly horrified at the stain left behind.

Sometimes it isn't necessary to say anything at all. The natural world speaks for itself and doles out its perfect lessons just fine.

Sid

He paces his bedroom with the idea of money on his mind. It's all about the money—whoever has it has power, not the politicians or holy rollers or even Nobel Prize–winning scholars. He's well aware that he's lived a privileged life in a gilded cage. But as for money, he couldn't care less! In fact, from this point forward he will refuse all allowances from his father. He's old enough now; therefore he will get a summer job pedaling the swan boats. Be self-reliant. Make just enough money to live on his own.

No, Sid considers money to be a kind of toxic mold. If you hold on to it too long, it poisons the atmosphere. In reality, it's just a piece of grimy green paper.

He wonders if he could casually toss it in a garbage bin. What would money look like if he dared to set it on fire? Perhaps, if he has the nerve, he might give away all his unearned cash to one of those buskers in Harvard Square. Or would that be too weird, or even worse, would it be perceived as condescending?

He doesn't know. But not-knowing only makes him restless like a caged bear. Of course he's not being held prisoner in his own home. His bedroom door is always open. So he'll go, right now, and take the subway into Harvard Square.

Homeless Woman

People shuffle past her call for spare change so she sings out, neon-graffiti loud, *Them that's got, shall get—*

Sid stops to listen as she rails on, belting out the next few lines, going deep as any canyon, dry as salt, as if she's rubbing bitterness into her own wounds.

He's half afraid of her appearance, the cliff-edges of her face, the dirty mess of her clothes and uncombed hair. But when she sings softly—*My Mamma may have, and my Papa may have*—he feels tears spring, fresh and hot, from his own eyes.

Then like an old coyote in a desert wasteland, she howls, letting fly all kinds of broken arpeggios into the refrain, *But God bless the child who's got his own—*

Sid's skin grows hot, then burning cold. She breaks off singing then, and shouts, *Do you hear me?* over and over at the passers-by bent on crossing Brattle Street, scaring them off like a flock of birds. And Sid doesn't know (heat rising in his ears) how or even if he should reply.

Yasmin

They go to the same elite high school. They live across the street from each other. He seems to have figured out that if he steps outside at precisely 6:15a.m. on a weekday morning he might see her waiting for her ride. And still, they've never really talked.

Today he's there, but unlike most days, he's brooding, staring off into space and doesn't even seem to see her, even after she slams shut her front door.

That bothers her, so she calls out, "Hey."

He calls back, "Hey." Then he halfwaves, halfnods, halfsmiles.

But she, on the other hand, is no longer amused by these timid forays into an actual, grown-up relationship. So she not only waves back but crosses the street and stands by his side.

"Hi, Sid. So what's new?"

Sid

Nearly three years to the day since they first hung out together, and Sid looks at Yasmin, tucked under his right arm, both of them huddled together under a ratty pink blanket. His heart bursts with joy. Not only are they together as a couple, but together, they have decided to join the Occupy Harvard movement.

The warmth of her body, the passion of their just cause! They, along with twenty-two other undergrad occupiers, have camped themselves in the Lamont Library Café, pledging to stay until planned staff reductions in Harvard libraries are reversed.

Together, they scan the morning's *Harvard Crimson*, heads tented under a blanket fold. There they are in the front-page photo, on the floor in front of the sofa. Just as they are now!

Sid reads: "More than twenty-three supporters of the movement gathered in the café to inaugurate the next phase of their protest..." Then his eye is distracted by the perfection of Yasmin's earlobe so close to him—how delicately it folds, how perfectly smooth and soft.

The two of them barely move, barely breathe. He overhears a couple of occupiers and hecklers having it out in front of the espresso stand.

"Libraries and librarians are important to a university and should be treated with more respect!"

"Hey, I agreed with the occupy movement overall until Harvard kids joined on the bandwagon. And sure, there are some genuine people involved, but this whole thing has been turned into a farce. You guys are sure inconveniencing yourselves by camping out on nice couches, right next to food and hot, caffeinated beverages. To stay at a café for a week—what a terrible sacrifice!"

"Yes, it is a massive sacrifice. Now I can't have sex with my girlfriend for most of next week."

"People have sex in Harvard libraries all the time, dude."

Sid and Yasmin don't look at each other. All he can think of is...*they do?...where?...how?*

Yasmin

For some unfathomable reason they haven't seen much of each other since the café occupation. She's been busy; he's been swamped. He told her in a hurried email that he joined crew, and he's out there slicing through the glassy early morning river before anyone else has gotten out of bed. One morning, secretly, she went out to watch him.

Now, this evening, she and her father have come to Sid's house, ostensibly for the fathers to discuss department politics. Sid and Yasmin have been left to themselves, and they sit side by side on the living room sofa. They can hear their fathers' heated conversation in the library. Yasmin listens to the cat walking out of the room, her nails ticking across the old oak floorboards as she, too, leaves them alone.

Sid, after an awkward silence, offers a bouquet of questions— *Would you like a glass of wine, or something to eat? Are you cold?* She finds this endearing. It is, at best, an amateur magician's trick to disguise his deep, abiding love for her.

She looks squarely into his eyes.

Then in a moment both thrilling and brash, all kinds of words fly between them like reckless acrobats performing miles above ground. He says, "I won't live my life tucked away in an academic bubble."

She says, "Then let's, both of us, teach in the worst New York City schools for the rest of our lives."

He says, "Brilliant. We can live on Staten Island and ride the ferry together to work every day."

"Or the other way around."

"Whichever. The important thing is, will you marry me on the ferry halfway between?"

The nakedness of that particular question startles them both.

Her hand lies so very close to his own. His hand moves closer.

She wonders what trembling of hers belongs to the cold and what to the quavering in her voice when she answers, simply, "Yes."

Ava

She yawns, mightily, at the point where Sid says, "I promise to love and blah, blah, blah until death do us blah, blah, blah." And then a little further on in the script, when he so earnestly says, "I do," Ava yawns again, interrupting the reverent, light-infested interior of First Parish Church where Sid and Yasmin are looking at each other in nervous adoration.

She just can't help herself. She's seen it all before. A hundred million times. She mumbles under her breath to the tear-stained second cousin of the bride twice removed, "I give them seven years, tops."

The second cousin twice removed glances over at Ava with a loopy smile and a drunken laugh. "I give them two. But what I wouldn't give for those 730 days, I'm telling you."

Yasmin

Yes, she knows how to cultivate roses. But how to work courage into the growing roots? How to give more room to the hips as they open up to him? In truth she has no idea about the daily maintenance of love and only dodges that terror by airing out the same answer over and over again, yes, in good faith.

She cries out, *Yes*, allowing for plenty of space and light in the garden as they mate for life, flavoring the blossoms with rain water and tears. She spreads the petals wide as if she's done it all her life.

Her tongue tastes the hidden question, "What will it cost?" And the skin all over her body answers again, *Yes*.

LEAVING
HOME

Siddhārtha

One day, a courier exclaims in the presence of the prince, "You must come out to the countryside!" He goes on to tell a glorious tale of how the grass in the woods has become a tender green and how, in the quiet, fertile ponds in the woods, great lotuses are unfolding.

Then, like an elephant too long confined in his stable, Siddhārtha has an irresistible desire to go there. Hence, once again, the king arranges for the entire kingdom to be rid of beggars, thieves, and the disfigured. The city sparkles with garlands and streamers. The king kisses his son on the brow and his gaze lingers over him as he says, sighing, "Go."

Only the rich, the young, and the beautiful are allowed on the streets that Siddhārtha drives through. As before, on his last expedition, people stop their daily activities to watch him as he passes by. Some praise him for the kindness of his glance, others exalt the beauty of his features, while still others glorify his exuberant strength. And all bow like willows before him.

But then, standing in their midst, a man appears whose body is afflicted with a loathsome-looking disease.

Siddhārtha sees this being, so different from the others, and gazes at him with stunned and sorrowful eyes. He asks his charioteer, "What is this man with a swollen belly? His emaciated arms hang limp. He cries pitifully and gasps for breath. See how he staggers and jostles the bystanders. Driver, what is this man? Has nature made him thus or is it by some stroke of chance?"

"My lord, this man knows the torment of sickness, and soon he will die. Yet he was once healthy and strong, like you. Indeed, sicknesses of many sorts weigh heavily upon this world."

"Will that be my fate, also?"

His driver nods and Siddhārtha begins to tremble like a moonbeam reflected in the waves of the sea. His heart quakes, like a bull at the sound of thunder. At once, Siddhārtha turns back to his palaces, his mind wrapped tight in an unshakable cloak of fear and confusion.

His driver races back to the palace, and all along the way, Siddhārtha plagues him with questions. "How is it that death is so near and yet human beings amuse themselves in a thousand different ways? How can it be that death is near and yet a human being takes to the highroads with a trivial song on his lips? How is it even conceivable that a human being who knows what death is seeks pleasure in the very hour of his anguish?"

But his driver has already said too much and he only delivers the prince in haste toward the king's pleasure garden where the king has ordered him to take his son. There, assembled hastily, a hundred beautiful maidens skilled in the arts of song and love greet Siddhārtha, their hands folded like lotus buds, awaiting the pleasure of the prince.

While for his part Siddhārtha frowns, his eyebrows knit together like corded vines. He stares off into the distance where the thought of death awaits behind every leaf and shadow.

For a little while, the women gaze at him, eyes opened wide with wonder. Then they stand closer, their minds absorbed in adoration wherein they seem to drink him in with eyes that remain unblinking, blossoming wide in ecstasy. Soon one of them feigns intoxication and unwinds the blue veil that binds her breasts; another draws near and whispers in his ear, "Deign to hear my secret, O prince." Yet another sings, "Listen, love, to the bees; they are roused and consumed by a burning ardor."

But the prince cannot be forced into frivolity. Beneath the sensual surfaces, he sees the true secret that has been withheld from him for so long: all is excrement, disease, and inevitable decay.

Not two weeks past this incident, Yasodharā gives birth to a beautiful child. Siddhārtha watches his infant son, Rāhula, at his mother's breast. It takes the child no time at all to find his target. Meanwhile, the royal seers swarm around the boy, one examining his foot and another the tiny crown of his head, each rushing to identify the thirty-two signs of a great birth. Yes, the top of his head has a crown-protrusion made of radiant flesh, round and circling clockwise. Yes, the palm of each hand has the impression of a thousand-spoked wheel. In addition, the soles of Rāhula's feet are as smooth and level as the breast of a tortoise's shell so that his feet will always be firmly planted. Furthermore, it is duly noted that Yasodharā has been at peace throughout her lying-in, that she has dreamed of a small white elephant wandering in her garden, that the birth was without pain. On and on, the list is predictably checked off. Their conclusion is clear: Rāhula has inherited all the marks of a great man.

Nevertheless Siddhārtha falls into an all-consuming misery. For every auspicious sign there still remains the fetter and bond of human frailty. And for every blessing bestowed on their royal family, death will, in the end, disown it. The city reeks of celebration, oblivious to true reality. Why is a beautiful child born only to grow old and sick and die? As he gazes at the perfect face of his sleeping son, he resolves to tackle any kind of austerity in order to understand.

Finally, one day, there arises within him a synchronized storm of resolve. For four immeasurable times and a hundred thousand kalpas, he has longed to fulfill the complete Perfections.[1] Right now, tonight, he will leave his palace life. He awakens his groom and tells him, "Bring the horse Kanthaka, and I will depart at once to attain that most noble place of deathlessness. Since my purpose is sure, most certainly my goal will come into view."

The majestic Kanthaka is brought forward. Siddhārtha embraces the stallion and speaks soothingly with a most intimate plea, as if they were about to plunge into the midst of a hostile army together, "Take me away from here, with speed, to the forest of the dharma."

The city gates, normally impervious to the strength of elephants, open easily of their own accord as Siddhārtha approaches. Soundlessly, horse and rider pass through. Siddhārtha, whose eyes are long like stainless lotuses born of mud, looks back at the city and he utters a lion's roar, "I shall not enter Kapilavastu again until I have destroyed old age and death!"

Kanthaka carries him a great way, far from villages and deep into the wild. When the sun finally peers between the eyelids of night, they arrive near a wood where pious hermits intermingle with sleeping deer, each without the slightest fear of the other.

Yasodharā

The next morning, when Siddhārtha's charioteer appears at her bedchamber door, she sees everything written on his face before he can open his mouth to explain. Siddhārtha has not gone for morning ablutions; he has not gone out to walk in the gardens. No, he has gone and abandoned his wife and son.

"Good friend of Siddhārtha, where is my beloved? Go bring him to me now. I will and must see him immediately."

She lets her combed hair fall; she lets her breasts ache. She lets everything golden be melted down to tears. Her beloved has gone to become a Buddha and she will not ever again look at the flower-decked bed where they lay as their hearts desired.

"Charioteer, do you not know that Siddhārtha and I have been married for innumerable lives, that we were first born in the animal world as wild rabbits and since that earliest incarnation, we two have never been apart? In every samsaric birth I have been his consort. Once we went as ascetics together to the forest. We happily carried out two children in our arms. Why then has he left me alone now? Is there anywhere in the world another woman so bereft?

"In a former birth we were tiny birds in a tender field, and our young one fell into the talons of a hawk. I well remember how Siddhārtha strove to save him. Why then does he leave his young son now?

"Once we were born as kinduras—halfhuman and halfbird. Does he not recall the nobleman that was out hunting and saw us, that fell in love with me and killed my beloved Siddhārtha in an attempt to win me over? I, however, refused to leave my dead husband. Only upon hearing my lamentations were the gods moved by my grief so that they restored him back to life.

"Am I not, again and always, his Yasodharā?"

The charioteer stands, mute, in front of her lamentations. He watches as she tears off her pearl and gemstone necklaces, her golden silks, the rings on her toes, the ornaments in her ears. Finally, she sits on the cold floor as if turned to stone.

The charioteer quietly departs, stepping backward into the full measure of his own, and indeed, the whole city's grief.

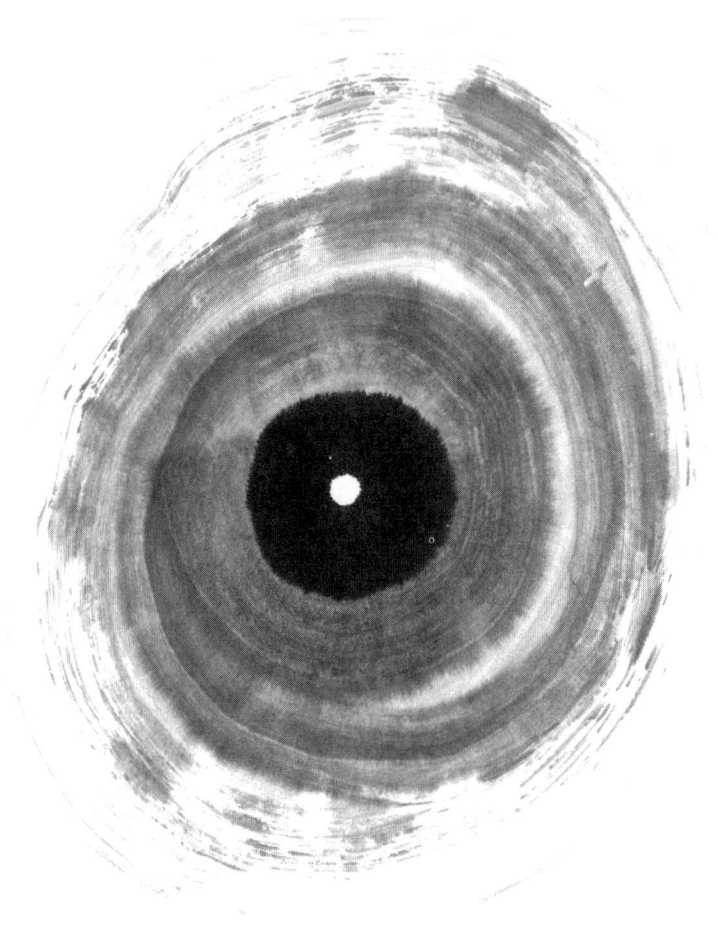

Cosmos

Dear one, I am an illusion of lapsed time, a veritable Houdini of name and form. Do you think you can withdraw from any part of me? If so, that's your first catastrophic flaw, leading to complete despair. Please know that I'll always meet you here, at the speed of the great unknown, and I can't miss.

Sudovsky

Housing is just far too expensive for young people these days. Would he have them, as they start their careers, living in a rat and cockroach infested one-room apartment in the Bronx? It doesn't make sense. Later on, when he's dead and gone, they can sell this house and live wherever they like in relative comfort. What good does it do to live in an urban war zone, where one's very life is at risk walking to the subway train? How will that help humanity?

No, he has urged patience, lobbied for reason. They are a young couple that needs their privacy—of course. So he has moved into the basement. For all practical purposes, the house is theirs. What does he need? A desk, a bed. Nothing more. Perhaps some floor space to stack up his books. That is all. He will not interfere. He will take his meals on campus. He will have a separate entrance built for himself at the back of the house.

Let them stay here and begin their teaching careers in Cambridge, a community they already know. With his influence, he has already found excellent positions for both of them. They will do well. They will prosper and be happy. They will live long and raise a family together. And he, Sudovsky, will bask in their joy. It is enough. It is more than enough.

Sid

Sid carries a shoulder bag with the latest pink copy of the *Financial Times* tucked up under his arm. He vaults down the front steps, practically singing to himself, I am a full-fledged adult. I have a wife. Look, look everyone, at the third finger of my left hand! It's official; I'm official.

He walks to Cambridge Rindge and Latin High School, rushing now to get to his first class in time. The people going in and out of doors (just like him) seem to move with the same rhythm, spring, and stride.

He can't help himself and smiles relentlessly. He arouses the sensations again, of Yasmin's skin last night and again this morning. So soft, so deep and warm.

At every corner the wet earth smells delicious. Trees intertwine their limbs, which excite the leaves. Far, far away the galaxy's spiral of stars explodes to glittering dust forged billions of years ago and also, just now, as ordinary traffic rushes to its climax and Sid is there, right there at the center of it all.

Yasmin

Years pass, even to those not looking. Seated side by side, they celebrate their fifth anniversary at the Epicurean Claw. While Sid peruses the menu card, she scans the restaurant's white rooms, the carved railings, the latticed entryway. Their elegant plates lie in wait for their gourmet food to arrive.

To us, she and Sid say to each other, and raise their glasses, while in her mind, she marvels at the trajectory of her life. If someone gives her a chair, she sits down. She has always been a good girl. If someone wants her to teach a seminar on medieval poetry, she teaches. If someone wants sex, she spreads her legs. And suddenly five years have passed. What if, when the script calls for our glasses to be raised, that is not what she had in mind at all?

A line from Eliot's love song comes to mind, no doubt inspired by the restaurant's decor: "I should have been a pair of ragged claws / Scuttling across the floors of silent seas."

Salad, cradled lobster, stuffed sole decorate the table. She glances at the next table where champagne leans against the side of a bucket, a baby in a crib.

"Would you like some?" Sid asks kindly, though to what he is referring is unclear.

Yasmin looks out the plate glass window where the sun deepens to a steely blue. It could have been described as beautiful; indeed, her whole life could be described that way. But what she would really like, she now realizes with some urgency, is for Sid to just talk to her, to tell her a story about magpies, or a drama going on at the high school. Anything. He could even tell her that he loves her. She wouldn't mind at all.

But instead, he asks, holding up the ragged, steamed tail of a lobster, "Is this one big enough?"

Sid

Ava points to his father, curled in a near fetal position in his bed. She hands Sid a damp cloth. "Wipe his forehead with this. The body temperature can swing wildly at this late stage."

Sid holds his father's right hand and wipes his father's brow, and kisses him lightly, the same way he kisses his infant son, Rāhula. Sid watches as this man who once terrified and enchanted him with his brilliant mind and clumsy love now labors for each breath. The professor's eyes struggle to open, and fail. He lies folded, as in a womb of transcendent pain. Faltering, Sid calls to him, "Daddy," using that childish term abandoned so long ago, "Daddy, I'm here. I'm here now."

His father's eyes open, see him, fix on him. Suddenly the breathing slows to an impossible length of time. Sid stares at his face, watching, listening intently for the chance of another breath. But no, no, that is all.

Three years after his father's death, Sid looks about him and sees that he hasn't really moved from his comfortable life, not even by a hair's breadth. Even though they sold the house in Cambridge and moved to this highly rated suburban town, so little has changed.

Today their tidy boutique town is celebrating a Fourth of July parade with firetrucks and last year's beauty queen, with streamers and candies and speeches. While Yasmin and Rāhula have gone on ahead to a prime viewing corner, Sid stays behind to help with the festival cleanup crew. He stands with a smile pasted at the front of his face, watching the tail end of the parade progress down Main Street.

Of course they had reasons for moving here—for its excellent schools wherein their beautiful young son, Rāhula, would have a chance to excel. But frankly, they've been worried about him being bullied because he is turning out to be so quiet and naive, and kind to a fault. Now they're considering home schooling as a way to protect the boy, also adding private Aikido lessons and kung fu.

Sid watches the mayor stand and wave from the back seat of a baby blue convertible. The mayor throws out fistfuls of candy, and the children lose their balloons in order to clamor after the treats.

After the mayor's car and the high school marching band, a dancing bear twirls in a sequined dress. For a moment, Sid believes it to be a real bear, a living beast trained to turn the other cheek and do a plié and pirouette. The bear bows to the children. The children scream. The squalling horns whip up the crowd to a near-hysterical good cheer.

Then Sid, for the first time since his father died, starts to weep with great heaving sobs.

He retreats from the crowd. Finding a spare broom, he starts to sweep confetti into heaps. Crows dive-bomb for spilled popcorn and kids run through his piles as if through autumn leaves. Vigorously he sweeps up every cigarette butt, candy foil, and errant feather. Hours pass this way until the street opens for traffic again. Finally, near dark, Sid shuffles the long way home, tears still streaming hot from his eyes.

Yasmin

The morning after the parade, she watches him pace the living room. At one point, he turns to her and asks, "Do you suppose this is all that it means to be a human being?"

Yasmin shrugs, brushing off, as best she can, the pain his pain inspires. In all honesty, she has wondered the same thing, but would rather not say so out loud. Together, they stare through triple-paned windows even though the parade has long since passed. In the distance they catch sight of a train heading west and they watch the rumbling wheels roll by. He sits with his legs folded and composes his hands.

Yasmin leans her head on his shoulder. This ought to be the very picture of happiness. They live in an enviable world. He teaches math at an elite high school and she teaches poetry at the university. They have a glorious child.

And yet, as the train pulls out of sight, she knows he imagines being on it. She strains to hear the train's progress on the iron rails, to see its exhaust fumes streaming away to the vanishing point or the breaking point, whichever comes first.

Ava

Ava always has a lot of work to do. So what else is new? Along with the everyday task of listening to everyone with patience, compassion, and at least a smidgen of curiosity, Ava engages in ongoing exposés of crook mythologies, a pet project of hers. Always, she has to hunt down the keys to unlock every prison cell built up around a word.

One day, while reading in the late professor's journals she came across the definition of the boy's name. Rāhula, it said, did not mean bond or fetter. Ha, Ava knew that eons ago, long before the boy was a glint in his father's eye.

She shouts into Sid's far-away mind, *Sid, are you listening? Even your father knew that the name Rāhula is a diminutive of Rāhu, the deity who swallows the sun or moon during an eclipse. It would have been a natural name for a beloved child. Names derived from stars or constellations are everywhere—these days all the best kids in the suburbs have them.*

In Ava's personal records (her perfect eternal memory) the moon, as it happened, was eclipsed at Rāhula's birth.

Sid, you were there. You named the boy. Don't you remember? You thought it to be original, regal even.

Then Ava whispers into Rahula's mind, *Rāhula, your name is avatar for a whole constellation eclipsing the moon. And I am Avalokiteśvara, which means I'm listening. Call me Ava, for short, and I will call you Rāhu, which doesn't mean bondage; it means one who swallows the moon for breakfast and spits out all the seeds.*

I'll sit by the window and unravel Houdinis from their chains while your beloved parents are otherwise engaged. If you need anything, call and I'll come tie your shoes, untie your fears, and mop up tears, or sort out all the dazzling, mirror-ridden trinkets of desire.

Call me Ava, which is avatar for true love, same as yours but with alternate stars.

Sid

Sid wakes up in a sweat, convinced that a burglar is trying to break in at the front door. He throws on a bathrobe and tiptoes out of the bedroom. On the way out he grabs Rāhula's baseball bat and holds it at the ready with both hands. He's a man, isn't he? He can handle it.

He stands behind the front door, listening for what may have been an hour. Finally, calmed more by exhaustion than anything else, he opens the door, looks around into the darkness, sees nothing, and is about to close the door and go back to bed when he sees a note tacked to the door frame.

Then, in an instant, he's on the phone dialing 911. To the phone operator on the other end, he explains, and then he has to explain again three or four times.

"Somebody tacked a note to my door. Yes. It was handwritten. It said, 'The Taiwanese Vampire Acrobats will kidnap you tomorrow.' No, I never heard of such a gang. But they spelled my name wrong. How can you spell Sid wrong? Sir, you spell Sid, *S-i-d*. They spelled it with a *C*. There's something really creepy going on here."

The phone operator laughs, actually laughs at him, and says, "There's plenty of crazies around, that's for sure, buddy." Then he yawns, insinuating that Sid's fears aren't half that creative.

"Call a friend," the operator says, "lock your doors. Just to be on the safe side."

Yasmin

Okay, Sid, so it's finally come to this. You want to know how many roads a man must walk down before you can call him a man. I'm not a man so don't ask me.

Before talking about how many roads or even calling the road a road, or a man a man, just consider this, Honey—how do you intend to nail down a path, let alone walk on it? I can just see you going down a bright-lit avenue with a knapsack of my poems, but leaving me behind. Sure. And I predict you'll be out of directions before you've walked past the Dollar Store.

So here are my terms: walk out that door and it's goodbye for good. And don't forget, your boy's downstairs. Before you go, tell him which road you've picked. Let him know how to find you when he asks why you're going. Write him a poem all by yourself. And maybe years later, he'll read your poem to his own child before he walks out on his wife.

I'm sorry. This isn't how I imagined our story would turn out. My man may turn out better because of a road and I might be better off being let down than led astray. Give me time. Thing is, poems usually have something in them—roads of all sorts. Take Frost's less-traveled walkabout. Look around. If you find the man you want to be, be careful how you call him. He may slip aside no matter how loud you holler. Or he may turn downstream of a flood no die-hard fisherman could follow. Even if you don't remember Robert Frost's poem, the main point is that he goes out and comes to a fork in the road and takes one that's never been walked before.

No, the poem doesn't tell you how to get there. But try this, Honey—drive downtown. Take the main road. Ask the first man you meet.

Sid

Heartache follows him as he wanders from room to room. At every step he is trailed by a perfect storm within the walls of his own head. As one overtaken by a tidal wave, he gasps for some shred of air to breathe. He is, eventually, going to die, as are Yasmin and Rāhula and all the others. Only the expiration dates remain unknown. For a week now he has stayed home unable to gather enough willpower to wade through the tasks of eating, brushing his teeth, going to work. He keeps thinking about that note from the Taiwanese Vampire Acrobats. He hasn't told

Yasmin about it, and a part of him knows better than to believe such nonsense. She'd only laugh.

He finds Yasmin digging weeds in the garden with the fury of an avenging angel. He stands at the screen door, watching.

"You could at least help me out here, you know," she says as she stabs at a dandelion root with enough force to smite a rock in two.

A flash of anger leaps like a lightning strike between them. That's it, he says to himself, and a moment later he has his jacket on, the car keys swiped off the table, and he's backing out of his immaculate driveway, steering onto the main road out of town.

Driving well over the speed limit, his mind spins wildly through bitter ruminations of he-said/she-said and reified memories of rights done wrong.

Then just as he rounds a curve, his car spins out of control. He turns the wheel hard but careens sideways through a hundred slick rewrites of his failure of a life. Hand-over-hand, he spins the car around four or five times until the vehicle finds the center of the road.

Sid breathes in mightily. And breathes out. He looks up to see the light ahead turn green. Just then, he has a pathetic insight, small but true: he realizes what it signifies to be alive as the light changes. It means *Go*.

Bear

For my daily bread, I turn the other cheek and do a plié and pirouette.

I used to pace a concrete park of lost, dispirited beasts, but at least it was on all fours. Now I perform dance moves and endure dreams of catching fish with feeble human hands.

MEDITATION

Siddhārtha

Siddhārtha wanders among the forest hermits, observing their austerities. He asks, "As I have never seen a hermitage until today, will you kindly explain your practices to me—what is your resolve and to what point it is directed?"

"Ours is the doctrine of renunciation. We live as birds that peck at seeds, or deer that nibble on withered grass. We coil our matted hair soaked in dung and offer oblations of sacred texts. We plunge into the coldest waters and dwell with the fish, our bodies scored by turtles, crabs, and stones."

"What does this achieve?" Siddhārtha asks.

"Bliss is obtained by the path of suffering. Therefore we eliminate our base desires in order to achieve paradise."

"This effort seems admirable. But, tell me, isn't this design another form of desire? And doesn't deliberate suffering create more suffering? Mind you, I can see that by your ascetic practices you could well ascend to the Tusita heavens, but the human race will still continue to turn and turn again in its agonies. How will your efforts, noble wanderers, help the rest of us?"

Yasodharā

His soft, untested feet have always been tender as lotus buds—so how will they ever walk upon a rough forest ground, at the mercy of indifferent heat and cold, punishing rains and droughts?

On what broken surfaces will he sleep at night? Accustomed as he is to lying on palace beds, massaged with aloe, sandal paste, and myrrh—how will his delicate body rest in the wild? Are there sufficient gods gathered around my beloved Siddhārtha, guarding him? Is he afraid of the woods where tigers roam? Does he even realize how the trees above his head weave despondent memories of me between their limbs?

How dare he leave us—this is what the forest must be whispering to him in warning. Indeed, our loss must weigh on a man who sits alone, not yet merged, not yet opened to his true self.

Avalokiteśvara

Years pass while she watches Siddhārtha fast. He starves to such a degree that he allows himself no more than a grain of rice and a single sesame seed each day. Finally he denies himself even that. And still, the great insight does not occur.

Avalokiteśvara, in tears, observes his self-abuse and inserts secret nourishment through the pores of his skin. Even so, his face, which had been a beautiful golden color, turns black. All thirty-two marks predicting his enlightenment disappear. So thin is he that if she were to place her hand on his stomach she could close her fingers around his backbone. His limbs, she observes bitterly, are like the jointed stems of creepers or bamboo, his backbone, like corded beads.

She looks close into his eyes, and they are sunk deep in their sockets like the gleam of water seen deep down at the bottom of the deepest well.

Siddhārtha

Near dying, Siddhārtha realizes that the suffering induced by fasting has only heightened his sense of self and brought him nowhere nearer the seat of awakening.

He recalls an experience from infancy when he had, quite naturally, sat beneath the shade of a jambu tree. There, at that time, his mind had settled into a state of deep calm and peace. If such a state could be attained as an innocent child, perhaps the enlightened way was equally close at hand.

Just then, Avalokiteśvara, in the form of a peasant girl, comes by, bows to him, and offers a bowl of rice milk. He drinks it all and bows deeply to her.

Once revived by the bowl of rice gruel, Siddhārtha comprehends that the middle path—not too much, not too little—is the true, unexcelled way. His five companion ascetics, however, observe Siddhārtha taking food and they say to each other, "It is Siddhārtha's vanity and weakness. Indeed, how shall he ever ascend to the Buddha seat now? A man in search of food only seeks comfort. Next he will want water to refresh and wash his forehead! Imagine! So we five must go elsewhere to learn the way to enlightenment. Surely we will not be able to obtain it from him. We were mistaken: he is a madman and a self-serving fool."

Siddhārtha maintains his own insight and with resolve, he goes alone to the Bodhi tree. He, the lion with the bearing of a swan and the gait of a supreme elephant, takes up the matchless, immoveable cross-legged posture with his limbs massed together like the coils of a sleeping serpent.

Mosquitoes buzz around his head, but he doesn't move. Demons with the faces of wild boars, tigers, bears, and lions tear through the inside of his brain, but he doesn't cry out. Beasts one-eyed, many-mouthed, three-headed, and armed with talons and teeth dance around him, but he takes no notice. Ash gray or tricked out with red spots, devils bristle with putrid odors. Siddhārtha ignores them and stays exactly where he is.

One demon lets loose a burning shower of red-hot coals, but they land as mere sparks at his feet and then burst into a shower of red lotus petals. Throughout all of this, Siddhārtha remains as he is, left leg folded over the right thigh; right leg folded over the left thigh. Eyes settled into the middle distance.

There he sits in absolute stillness, quiet as a mountain peak and shining like the moon rising out of a bower of clouds. All the birds and wild beasts refrain from speech. And the forest trees, when struck by the wind, refuse to rustle with even the slightest sound.

Crow

Nightfall. Nothing moves. Time slows to eternity as we roost
for the night in a city park, clustered on a branch overhanging a
garbage bin.

Though it's been said we're smarter than some college
undergraduates, little good that will do as we sleep, blind to the
perils of darkness.

Sid

He drives right past the Dollar Store but stops in the next block at Boutique Natural Foods. He hasn't packed so much as an energy bar from home. On entering, he reads a sign in the window— THE ZERO ZEN DIET: 7 Steps to Enlightened Health!

Sid asks the emaciated young man in dreadlocks behind the counter, "What's this Zen diet all about?"

"It's an elimination diet, man. Totally new. I'm on it now. You start with nothing. Three days, nothing but water. That's the zero part. Then you move on to green shakes and supplements made from rare seeds straight out of the Amazon rain forest. Here's a pamphlet. It's a bit pricey, but worth every penny."

"What does it cure?"

"Well, to be honest, I got a massive headache at the beginning, but then things smoothed out amazingly after that. I guess that's the Zen part. Love it. Look here in the pamphlet and you can see what it's good for—things like cancer, depression, anxiety, fibromyalgia, arthritis—you know, that sort of thing."

Sid sighs and empties his wallet. "Who knows, I guess I'll give it a try."

Yasmin

She feeds and sings to the child, paces the room, bursts into tears, then sweeps up Rāhula and tells him they are going on an expedition to the petting zoo.

They could, she resolves, still have a life and carry on. All they have to do is face the day, the hour, the moment, and then move on to the next.

At the petting zoo, she says, "Rāhula, look. Look at the weary mother deer, look at her beloved Bambi." Naturally, nowhere is there any sign of Bambi's dad, not in real life or in fables, either one.

Near them a woman carries a hydrocephalic child, his heavy head askew and his lips twisted and wet with drool. Together the two mothers arrive at a clearing, where, surprisingly, an old-fashioned carriage waits, pulled by two horses. The coachman tips his hat and sweeps open his hand, "Would you ladies care for a ride?"

They both say yes. The horses' bells jangle, the coachman snaps his whip in the air and off they go into another era, any era will do.

They are a pair of mothers and babes going for a ride against the brutality of normal life. And who is to blame? They manage to laugh, more for the sake of their children than themselves. They point out pretty views with gritty pain caught behind their eyes. One croons to her child. The other calls out, "Look, we are riding in Cinderella's Coach!"

The sickly child rolls his head. Rāhula sucks his thumb. The coach rises over the hillside and skirts a deep ravine.

"Once more around the park, shall we, ladies?" the cheerful coachman calls.

The mothers clear their lungs and shout out just ahead of weeping, "Why not? Yes," and again, "Yes."

Sid

Back on the main road, while doing his best to mind everybody's road rage and ignore his own, he sees a hand-lettered billboard spelled wrong—BUDDAH'S STATE LINE SCRAP→ THIS EXIT.

Buddha ought to end in a -*ha*, not an -*ah*. He's still his father's son, after all.

So Sid follows the free-drawn arrows off the highway leading to a field of weeds, all the while chewing out the proprietor in his head, *Words ought to be floated out into the world with more respect!* He parks and slams his door. He marches past stacked radiators and copper pipes.

But when he gets to the office door, Sid stalls. His anger shifts to confusion and doubt. Why, exactly, is he here? To correct the spelling on a sign?

A voice calls out from inside, softer than he would have thought possible in a junkyard, "Come on in. We don't tend to print out invitations."

Sid enters and scans the chaos across the room—matchbox cars heaped on a file cabinet, twisted lengths of copper wire, lead weights heaped in a corner, a fake peacock feather wedged into the side of an old picture frame.

"So, what can I be doing for yah?" The man leans over his desk. Panicked, Sid stammers, "I'm looking for..." The proprietor looks him up and down and replies, "You need doors? We got doors. You need windows? We got those too." Siddhārtha nods stupidly. Buddah slams his hand on the desk. Dust flies.

"Okay! Now we're getting somewhere. For outside doors, take the path that runs between the angle irons and hubcaps. Inside doors are in the barn. Windows, if you need 'em, are just about everywhere."

Boston Public Garden

A man without a name asks of the forested grove, May I come in?

Leafless beech trees stand in austerity; black crows fly overhead, and he asks all of them, Will you teach me?

By way of answer, the world's eye, the sun, overturns the collective bowl. Without options to pick or choose, he receives his portion of warmth. He finds a quiet place wherein he sits on an empty park bench facing the pond.

One of the crows observes from her perch on one of the highest tree limbs—here's a new disciple recently arrived. Fascinated, the crow watches this young man who begins thus, with all the keen-eyed hunger of one of her own kind.

Sid

He pulls his hat down over his ears and nearly over his eyes. He blows on his hands, first one and then the other. Mist rises from his breath, and also from the grass as the sun slowly has its wide effect.

He sits hunched over himself with his shoulders caved in. Now what? He stares down at his shoes, then at the grass that has been trampled under the shoes, then at the frost still clinging to the blades of grass, then at the light reflected on the frost.

Silently he vows to himself that he will not move from this spot until he understands something, anything. He doesn't need to know who he was before his parents were born—just what it is that he's supposed to do next. That would more than suffice.

Ava

"Sid, sit up straight! Oy vey! How many times have I told you that with posture like that your breathing is compromised and by extension, your immune system and overall good health will suffer?"

Sid looks up, startled to see his old nanny dressed in a dark green city park uniform, carrying a paper sack. He smiles, with a tear clinging to the edge of his left eye. "Ava, I haven't seen you in ages. How are you?"

"I'll bet your back hurts, yes?"

Sid nods.

Ava shakes her head, clucks her tongue at him. "Sid, you should eat something. Look at you, skin and bones. Are you hungry?"

"Ava, what are you doing here?"

"You should know me by now, Sid. In my spare time I like to do volunteer work. Today I'm riding the swan boat back and forth, making sure no one falls out before getting to shore. So?

Don't look at me like that. What else should I be doing? Here, take this." Ava passes him a steaming falafel wrap, oozing with hummus. "Eat."

She watches him take a bite and then she watches him put the rest aside. "What am I going to do with you?" she asks. "If not for me, you'd starve."

She shakes her head and without waiting for a reply (obviously it was a rhetorical question; the boy has to chase his own demons), she heads off for the next load of passengers waiting to board one of those kitschy fiberglass swans. What she doesn't have to deal with! It beggars this poor bodhisattva's imagination.

Yasmin

I wait for the cue in the music where he comes back to me and I step aside to open the door. I've always known that my life isn't a dance floor and there are no choreographed moves. It may turn out that the time between our moves will be light years apart, or not even coincide, but whenever it does arrive, I have no idea how I will proceed. The door might find itself slammed in his face.

And yet I hope to place my next step in a line of direction that permits all of us to pass through.

Sid

Dreams, so many phantom lives lived—they alight in his mind like birds on a branch. Singly or in a crowd, ideas scan a horizon worn smooth of name and form, time and space, cause and effect.

Little by little, his mind grows weary of its two-bit cabarets and instead aligns itself to the tempo taken up by his surroundings—a small creature rustling under a nearby bush, distant laughter, midtown traffic noise.

He recalls things he shouldn't be able to recall—his mother whispering his name to him on the day of his birth, *S-s-s-s-i-i-i-i-i-i-i-d*, like the sound of a cooling breeze. He even remembers, as if it had happened to him, the terror of a tiny bird snatched up in the talons of a hawk.

One by one, thoughts and memories step off from the high branches. Each one of his exhalations drifts down to the end of itself. Anticipated pain is unbound, the shield of anger released, and even the odd moments of calm are given away, again and again, to the ground.

Gossips

We, personally, would never sit on hot coals, absorbed in meditation in a public park all day and all night. We would, however, be happy to give running commentary to those of you that do.

Sid, you just try to endure the biting chorus of our high-pitched laughter tightening into a noose around your neck. Your eyes will start to bulge out of your head. Your head will spin and your throat will be squeezed of every conceivable thirst.

We dare you to not join in with us, to just proceed with sitting still. Receive without moving the barbs, the famous foolish names being bandied about, the titillating facts.

The truth is, we are only hungry ghosts, eager to know if it's really true—is it possible to sit bare to the heart of a burning question and become, once and for all, alive?

Sid

He sits rooted to the iron city bench, riveted as completely as the bolts holding his seat together. For hours night shadows perform silent movies under a street lamp. A cool breeze wraps itself around him like a scarf.

Just then, a solitary rabbit hops lightly across the grass. The rabbit pauses to turn and look at him. His eyes, this close. Sid's eyes, just as close. Though they are of different species, they recognize each other. All the dots connect. And then the dots disappear.

This doesn't seem to surprise either of them. Two sentient beings gaze at each other at the shimmering gate of dawn. The morning star picks the lock, and leaves them as they are, open and shining free. He looks up and sees a star. Instantly, city gates and cerebral chains crumble. He and the star both fall together into what feels like a great ocean of being. Sid marvels at the brilliance of this momentary world. Looking about him, he sees glistening beings going to work, the tips of every blade of grass brushed alive by the glow of streetlights, each reflecting the universe, just as it is.

Just so, just now, it is a clear, bright day. He smiles. All the stars in the universe say, *Yes!* And precious beings everywhere turn as one, nodding in complete accord.

Morning Star

(from somewhere in the instantaneous universe)

The morning star looks down and sees it all happen in 3-D, High Definition real time—Sid cut free of the phantom iron chain strung between his shoulder blades and his high-stakes, demonic dreams.

Like the greatest Houdini of all time, the Enlightened One has released the leaden bar over his own eyelids and opened his eyes wide. And he has seen the morning star. Finally.

"Took you long enough to look up," the star says.

"Took you long enough to rise," Sid says right back.

RETURN

Buddha

In the 103rd year of the Eatzana era, at the dawning of the full moon of Katson, the perfect nature of the universe breaks over him at once and he blossoms fully as the Awakened One.

When this great event takes place, ten thousand worlds sway in wonder. And all the trees of every world sprout branches loaded with fruits and flowers. Five sorts of lilies bloom spontaneously. At that moment no living creature gives way to anger and no one suffers any sort of disease. Humans and beasts arrive together in one accord. Rivers suspend their wandering and elephants trumpet his great enlightenment in full harmonic chorus.

Then he hesitates. To open his mouth, he knows, would divide the world in two again. To step away from the Bodhi seat would be to leave complete stillness in the midst of the most perfect harmony.

Cicadas call. A rabbit pauses in the clearing, chewing on a

mouthful of grass. A multitude of crows fly off from the highest branches of the pipal tree, leaves chatter beneath them—all one song.

And now here come two traveling merchants with an offering of food. He smiles. Are they not, each one of them, rising together in the morning dew? Are not causes and conditions always appearing—and disappearing, just so? Is not all of this the supreme unexcelled display of the middle way? This teaching brims from his mouth as he rises to greet the passing merchants. One look is enough to see the suffering and need in their faces. He will meet them there.

As he sets out from the seat of enlightenment, he considers who might be open to receive the subtle yet profound illumination. Then he recalls the blossoming of the lotus. Among the blue and white lotuses that flower in a pool, there are some that stay under water, others that rise just barely to the surface, and still others that grow so tall that their petals are not even wet. And in this world, the Buddha reflects, so are there good and evil people; some with sharp minds and others with minds that are dull; some will understand and others will not. But he should consider the lotus that opens under water as well as the lotus that displays its great beauty high above the muddy surface of the world.

Therefore he sets out from the seat of enlightenment to offer guidance to all, as best he can. He recalls his five former companions. They were his partners in austerity, each one of them endowed with virtue, intelligence, and energy. Their minds are pure, having little dust on their eyes. They will be able to perceive his first Dharma-teaching and will not become annoyed at hearing it. He will head for Deer Park at Ṛṣipatana, near

Vārāṇasī, where they have long struggled, so near to death, for the true insight.

The Five Disciples

He enters Deer Park and even from a distance they recognize him, and say to each other, "Do we not know this man, walking toward us? Is he not the one whose austerities used to astonish us, and who, one day, revolted against our grave self-discipline? If his mortifications did not show him the way to supreme knowledge then, how can his thoughts profit us today when he is clearly swayed by greed and cowardice? Let us not go and meet him, or rise when he approaches. Let us not relieve him of his cloak or of his almsbowl; let us not even offer him a seat. 'No,' we will say to him, 'All the seats here are taken.'"

But the nearer he comes to them, the more uncomfortable they feel. They are seized with a great desire to rise from their seats, like birds frantically trying to escape from a cage under which a fire has been lit. Finally they break their resolve and rise as one. They run to the Blessed One. They take his almsbowl and cloak. They offer him a seat and bring him water to bathe his feet.

Yasodharā

At first she refuses to meet him. He deserted them without warning, and now he has returned to Kapilavastu as the supreme Enlightened One, the Buddha himself. But is he not also Siddhārtha—softhearted and doe-eyed as he always used to be?

From her bare window she sees him arrive with twenty thousand holy men, and to every one of them, he is the Supreme

Being. She alone recognizes the man that is her husband. She watches, unseen by him, as he goes begging for alms with his retinue. She knows his step, his posture, his hands that curve around a bowl. She recognizes his fragile heart, his overlong limbs, as subject to cause and effect as anyone else's would be.

The others believe he is divine. But how can there be a fixed and endlessly perfected enlightened being? How can it ever be so when nothing and no one is permanent in this world? The true nature of reality, of the universe itself, is constantly changing, losing its balance and changing again.

However, she can see for herself that enlightened *being* is taking place right now. She watches him greet each person with humble grace and sincerity. Though he has given away all worldly possessions, including herself, she sees that there is something within him that is new. There is a certain glow, as if his face resembled gold. She will, she decides, test the quality of that gold.

"Look, Rāhula," she says to her son, "over there is the father you never knew, the one who left us. Go and ask him now for your true inheritance. Go and say respectfully that, as you are now the crown prince of this kingdom, destined to succeed your grandfather on the throne, you wish to become possessed of the property that will fall to you as your rightful inheritance."

Buddha

Like beings of pure gold, they approach. He watches Yasodharā push Rāhula forward on his own. Buddha looks upon the slender, pure limbs of his wife and recalls all the many lives they lived together in which she had freely given away her eyes, her flesh, her heart and head, tirelessly, life after life, for his sake. He bows deeply to them, overfilled with love, compassion, joy, and equanimity.

The boy, nervous yet thrilled, bursts out, "Father, give me my inheritance!"

"Beloved Rāhula, I have no worldly goods, but I have something far more excellent: an imperishable inheritance, both unborn and never dying. I can offer you the life of a contemplative. Rāhula, do you know the function of a mirror?"

"Yes. It is to reflect."

"In the same way, Rāhula, the functions of your eyes, ears, nose, tongue, body, and mind are to be undertaken with contemplation, with reflection. Whenever you are about to take action, reflect. 'What is this present moment reality? Is it genuine or is it a phantom creature created out of mind or heart's desire? Will my actions harm or assist?' In evenness and harmony, inquire into the nature of true reality in this way, and your precious inheritance will not only never expire but will increase throughout the kingdom of all sentient beings."

Rāhula looks up at him with eyes much like the Buddha's own. Love passes between them in an instant, and then Rāhula, in a high, squeaky voice, asks, "Are you my father or are you the Buddha?"

"Dearest Rāhula, all that I am is yours, right here, right now, so that I may assist in your awakening."

Avalokiteśvara

Many years pass and Buddha's teachings draw hundreds upon thousands of men to hear it, like moths to a flame, but

Avalokiteśvara, with just one of her thousand eyes, can easily see who longs to be there and thirsts to awaken as well. All women are kept outside, and none are granted permission to ordain.

Finally Avalokiteśvara, having slipped into the body of Buddha's aunt, leads five hundred mothers, wives, and daughters of Kapilavastu to remedy this injustice. Together, they arrive at the forest grove where the master instructs his many monks. "Beloved One," she says, "as you have taught that all sentient beings have Buddha-nature, do not we, as women, also have the capacity to learn and attain it? These women here beside me know the fleeting joys and endless sorrows of this world. Will you grant them permission to enter the sangha that grows around you? Their embroidered veils weigh heavily upon them; their diadems, bracelets, and necklaces bind. Here before you are women of earnest piety, eager to accept the wisdom of the Four Noble Truths and the practices of the Eightfold Path.[2] Will you allow it?"

This she asks on three separate occasions and each time the favor is denied.

Avalokiteśvara's eyes fill with tears, but she will not accept defeat. She and all the other women cut off their beautiful black hair. They put on ascetics' rags. Then they set out on foot, once more, to the place where enlightenment is taught, inherent to all sentient beings.

Covered with dust and pierced through with weariness, the women put their case before Ānanda, cousin and close disciple of their beloved teacher. To all of them, the Buddha's error is clear. Ānanda goes to him and respectfully reminds the Awakened One of his own teaching, "Beloved One, it is as you have always taught us…"

Compassionately, Ānanda recalls for him the wisdom Siddhārtha received from Avalokiteśvara, who had nursed him and brought him up with utmost tenderness from the day his mother died. Had not she and Yasodharā and so many other women already modeled the perfect disposition of a Buddha?

At last, the Beloved One's misgivings are overcome, and women are admitted, for the first time in the history of the world, as devoted members of the assembly.

Buddha

Before the vast assembly, he says, "Yes, there is a remedy for illness, available to all of us—it is received by saying into each broken name and form one indivisible word. What is it?"

He pauses a moment before answering the question himself, "It is just now, as we talk and listen to each other, that the medicine begins. Do you hear it?"

The leaves of the forest trees whisper; the multitude sighs.

He continues. "Furthermore there is a remedy for aging—it is attained by stepping off the edge of space on a single universal breath."

And then he pauses again, before adding, "It is just now, as we turn to each other, and extend ourselves. Do you see it? And, Dear Ones, there is a remedy for dying too. Life is sustained beyond time by letting the heart out of its cage, which in turn turns cause and effect to shimmering dust and streams us all into *being*. Do you understand?"

He pauses again, this time for a very long while. Then he reaches out, picks up a small blossom at his feet, and holds it aloft. For one meditation period, then two. Even as the sun

Crow

As full and sated as I am, I cannot appreciate my current state without first celebrating the love of my life—my last meal, and yours, too—wherein, ultimately, you have become me, which is heartwarming, because really, this is a tight embrace for both of us, isn't it?

Rabbit

Ever since I was borne so far into you (it was—and still is—a phenomenally rich stew) I finally understand for the first time how twenty-five cents can equal a quarter. And I wonder at how profound that is, like unconditional love, how intimate and selfless, how true.

Yasmin

She's in the middle of packing Rāhula's lunchbox and fishing out money from the bottom of her purse for his science project fee when Sid calls.

He says, "Yasmin, now I see it. A single flower equals a hundred rabbits. Everything is equal. Three times three equals zero! Ten thousand times fifty-seven equals zero!"

"Really," she says, dryly. He's been gone all night who knows where, and this is the first thing he has to say? Really? Rāhula is standing at her side—they have to get going if he's going to catch the school bus. But she's so relieved that her husband is still alive, she asks, "What does that mean, exactly? Math is your game, not mine."

"It means everything is complete, just as it is! I am riding on a swan boat, stretched out on my back looking up at the sky and I can see that the sky is blue, and I am talking to you!"

"Okay," she says, and now the anger and resentment come back, color rising to her face. "Good for you. So what are you going to *do* about it?"

"Come home," he says, and adds softly, "if I may."

That just about moves Yasmin to tears but she forges on, even as her voice quavers, "What I'm saying is since you've been gone things haven't exactly been easy. For one, the tea kettle broke."

"I'll fix it."

"And your department head called, wondering when you're coming back to work. But before you do anything else, check in with Rāhula. He needs help with his math. And by the way, just when you think the problem's been licked, the raccoons went on a rampage in the yard last night. So the pretty little Zen garden you made last year has been trashed, but you can take that on later. Look, I can't talk long. I have to get Rāhula on the bus and then meet with some of my students. But Honey—," Here she hesitates. If he had been standing in front of her she might have hit him. She can almost hear the slap of her hand on the side of his face. As it is, she swallows hard, then says, opening to the possibility, "It will be good to have you back again."

"I'll be right there."

Sid

He hadn't planned on the beauty of this broken world. But as he glances out the kitchen window to the backyard, he embraces this ordinary view as music to his ears. Never could he have imagined.

Sorting through his tool chest in search of a right-headed screwdriver, he feels the middle way, the reconciliation of his hands, one to the other and to their task. What is the sum total of all that remorse, love, and loss?

The heft of a broken teapot. The torque of the screwdriver tightening a loose screw. All of it—precious. Again, he glances through the window, this time to see a rabbit chewing on a mouthful of grass. Even from where he stands he can hear and feel the rabbit's teeth tearing through the greens.

What a view. The colors are astonishing, almost too grave and serene to bear! Memories, errands, and events appear and disappear. The usual ghosts pass through his mind—they too come and go. But prevailing behind all of it, and also closer than the eye can see, that clear blue field of sky.

He comes to the living room and sees his beloved son, Rāhula, slouched like an overcoat across the sofa, his bare feet dangling over the edge, no doubt cold.

His father pauses in the doorway. "Rāhula, I'm home again."

Rāhula raises a hand halfheartedly without turning around.

"Rāhula, are you cold?"

Rāhula shakes his head, *no*, but doesn't take his eyes off the TV.

"Son, your mother said that you need help with your math. I can help you now. Understanding basic fractions isn't all that hard. If you think about the denominator as being the constant, wide-open field, and the numerator as the changeable…"

"Dad. You're interrupting! This is the Transformers series—my favorite show."

"Sorry." Love wells up in an instant. He scoots in to sit next to his son, gently positioning the boy upright and straightening his spine by putting his arm around him, just so. Together they peer into the TV screen. "What's happening right now?" he asks his beautiful son.

"It's complicated, Dad. But see, those are the Decepticons—that means the bad guys that want to control everybody. They're greedy, and they're so busy going after other people's stuff, they don't even see what's right in front of their noses! See that little crow up in the tree? That's actually the boss of the good guys. In a minute, she's going to caw, really, really loud. That's the signal for all the good guys to wake up. Then everybody transforms. There's a huge face-off…"

"So I take it you've seen this before?"

"Sure, Dad, loads of times!" Then Rāhula burrows into Sid's chest, and Sid holds him there, like a momentary flash of sheer perfection.

Yasmin

Curled up on the sofa with sweet chai tea within arm's reach and a pile of poems beside her, she takes the next student's poem from the stack, three pages, single-spaced. Why oh why, she wonders, do aspiring poets equate heaps of words with high art?

Quickly she makes her notes in the margins: *Pay attention to punctuation, grammar, spelling. Watch out for run-on sentences and mixed metaphors.* She circles word after word and appends with the commentary: *know the difference between live and dead words.*

She pauses. Something encouraging must be said as well. She knows from her own experience that usually one's weakest point is also, given the right circumstances, the strongest. In her own case, her ever-constant willingness to throw herself into life with a hearty *Yes!* has delivered more bruises than promises. But the result has been a life of richness and profound joy. Not joy according to the slogans of self-help manuals. Rather, it is a joy caught up in the full embrace of glorious mayhem.

At the end of the student's three-page poem, she writes, *The emotion here is strong. To deliver emotion with an agenda, however, is to deliver dead words. Don't be attached to your feelings, but use them as raw energy to plumb the depths of what truly is. Allow your words to be filled with wonder, please.*

She picks up the next poem. Oh good, a short one. She smiles. This young author is not what anyone would peg, at first glance, as a poet. Broad-chested, muscled, and so large overall that he looks like an ogre in a child's chair at their seminar table. In reality, he's painfully shy. Each one of her students, such precious gems.

She reads,

once I
wrote a poem
about happiness.
nobody liked it
so I threw it away.

Naïve, yes, but she will have to fight to reflect his artistry back to him, encourage him to take up all the space of being alive. What a job it is to be a poet! Does anyone have any idea?

Sid

"Is *one* really the beginning?" he says, pausing to take in the scope of this year's freshmen class. That old adage, how time flies, comes to mind. Even after the shocking sum of forty-five years teaching math at Cambridge Rindge and Latin, he still looks forward to meeting each new student body. Student body! Look at them—a mass of youth, beauty, distraction, disquiet, and vitality. What a joy to be alive in this world—if only they knew. Hopefully, through the lens of mathematics, he will steer them toward that insight.

"What assumptions are we making," he asks, "when we package some arbitrary appearance as isolated, as *one*? For example, we might be better off and wiser to refer to ourselves as an infinitude, a superorganism, a fluid, ever changeable conglomeration of lives. Did you know that your 'body,' right now, is being shared with several hundred microbial species, each with its own agenda and expiration date? To ask the question, *What am I?* invites an infinite range of answers. And all of them would be wrong.

"So then, is one ever the real beginning of anything? And what about zero?

"If you multiply ten thousand by zero, the answer is zero. If you divide ten thousand by zero, you get infinity. What power, what range! Our normal way of thinking is turned on its head by this little zero. Why?"

He pauses, allocating time for the uncomfortable silence in the room. He knows they expect to be fed information, not to be caught offguard by impenetrable questions. After forty-five years of teaching, he also knows there's value in allowing for this sort of silence. It fosters a healthy habit of inquiry and independent thinking. He smiles, changes tack.

"Here's another question. What did the zero say to the eight?"

"Nice belt you have on there!" a voice calls out from the back of the lecture hall. A few students laugh. A ripple of relief spreads through the room.

"Excellent! And your name is?"

"My name's Ava, but you can call me Zero for short."

He does a double-take and tries to see where her voice is coming from, but it's darker in the back rows and he doesn't see so well as he used to. Laughter spreads across the hall. "Very good, I see we already have an enlightened listener in the audience! This bodes well for the coming year. So let us, for the purposes of this class, assume we all share the same last name, the common denominator of zero."

He smiles broadly as the students whisper among themselves, *You can't have zero in the denominator...it's not allowed...*

"Yes. If we divide anything by zero the entire foundation of logic and mathematics falls apart. Dividing by zero just once would allow us to prove anything whatsoever—say, for example, that Winston Churchill is a carrot.

"Meanwhile, in the phenomenal, moment-to-moment world it is helpful to use our differentiated, provisional names, yes? Therefore my numerator is expressed by the name Professor Sid, and yours must be Ava, back there in the last row. Hopefully, I'll learn the rest of your names in short order.

"Okay! Our class is now officially up and running. Tomorrow we'll move on to the origins of zero as a bold and brave concept for the inconceivable, first explored in ancient India, and if all goes well, we'll hit number one sometime next week."

DEATH

Siddhārtha

After forty-five years instructing all who care to listen, he sees the time approaching when his body will drop away. In the presence of his disciples he reclines on his right side, pillowing his head on his folded arm and stretching out his legs. The birds refrain from their music and sit with their bodies relaxed, as if fixed in a trance. The trees, with restless leaves unstirred by breezes, shed discolored flowers, as if weeping.

His voice emerges like a cloud and he says, "It is not fitting to grieve in the hour of joy. Despair is out of place.

"I am not the remedy. Just as a man does not overcome disease by the mere sight of a physician, so is he who does not overcome suffering by the mere hearing of these words.

"Even if you were to look at me for a hundred thousand eons, as if looking at someone divine, you would be grasping at appearances. You would increase the web of ignorance and delusion, bound and blind, unable to see the true, original Buddha.

"If you wish to break through the wall of life and death, make a firm resolve and shine a light, dear ones, unto to yourselves."

Trees

They both dance in the same direction, their eyes fixed on each other as they practice their beloved tango. Past and future become a blur. And who cares anymore about how to define the present tense?

She listens with acute kindness as he says, "Shall we have another go?"

STATEN ISLAND FERRY

The ancient ferry, free for all, slides into terminal beginnings, metal on metal. Linked chains collapse and people stream on board *en masse*—in tailored suits, journeyman work clothes, flip-flops, and high heels. The tourists arrive in a jumble, parents in a rush, too late to be young again, and artists stand absorbed, categorically, in being alone.

Once on board, all lean over the rails and peer into the churning water, mesmerized. They ask of each other, *Is it, are we, moving yet?* One elderly man knows this conundrum like the rutted road in water that it is. *Aren't we always?* He rides comfortably inside the question and smiles to himself.

He misses his wife, taken by cancer two years ago. Long, long ago, they had promised to be married on this boat, but the plan went awry, as plans tend to do. He watches the waves. The movement plays all the way to the horizon. And the chorus of accompanying sounds—gulls, humans, horns, water—is almost too beautiful to bear.

Passengers

On the upper deck of the ferry, an old man rests on a bench and as we walk by he catches our eye and holds us in his gaze. Instantly all of us melt inside and we can go no further. We draw near, and then see that he is in pain, maybe even dying. How can this be? How can anyone ever undone by sudden love distinguish between such boilerplate words as grief and joy?

While someone calls 911, this dear man looks at us, and we take our seat by his side.

He says, "I'm no one special. Just passing through."

"How can we help you?" we ask, while in our hearts we also mean to say, *Please love us*.

He smiles and says, "Today, I see, is a beautiful day."

We nod as if we understand, only knowing that we are being held by something bright and wordless in his eyes.

Then he doubles over, about to vomit, and starts to say, "I think it was something in the hot dogs—see if you can find—"

We find a few flimsy baskets, paper-thin, and hold them, one after another, beneath his face as he heaves. Very weak, he rests on his side. We sit at his feet and wipe his eyes, his nose and mouth.

He smiles slightly, and says, with difficulty, "Thank you. Not much time. I've decided. From now on, instead of saying *goodbye*, I'll say thank you. Thank you."

Then, with his last exhalation, he whispers these words one more time.

And ever since that day, we passengers carry on as best we can—some of us dance, fall in or out of love, complain, or pose for posterity with the waves behind us—and as we try to do the right thing, moment by moment, the ferry moves, almost imperceptibly, along.

ACKNOWLEDGMENTS

For my early readers, I am indebted to Sarah Flygare, Geri Larkin, Lee Teverow, and Jerry Maden for their careful, keen-eyed wisdom. For the luxury of time and space to write at critical junctures during the development of this work, my deep appreciation goes out to Soapstone and Hedgebrook, and Diane Walker for her generous gift of two weeks in a cottage on Shaw Island. For their partnership in creating this book, for bringing such wise and extraordinary art and design to *Sid*, I humbly thank artist Linda Davidson and graphic designer Katrina Noble. I am forever in awe of you. For believing in *Sid* from the beginning, for shepherding its development and fighting for its unique character in the publishing world, I bow in gratitude to my editor, Andy Francis. Special gratitude goes out to all those that make up my Dharma home in the Golden Wind Zen Order. And finally, for my family's enduring love, the engine that drives all, may my love echo back endlessly to all of you. Thank you.

ENDNOTES

1 The Perfections (*Pāramitās*):
   Generosity
   Precepts (Conduct)
   Perseverance (Patience)
   Effort (Energy)
   Samadhi (Meditation)
   Wisdom

2 The Four Noble Truths:
   Life is *duḥka* (suffering born of discontent).
   There is an origin of *duḥka*.
   Therefore, it is possible for there to be a cessation of *duḥka*.
   The Eightfold Path is the means to that cessation:
   Right View
   Right Thinking
   Right Speech
   Right Action
   Right Livelihood
   Right Diligence
   Right Mindfulness
   Right Meditation

BIBLIOGRAPHY

Armstrong, K. (2001). *Buddha*. New York: Penguin.

Bigandet, P. (1911). *The Life or Legend of Gaudama*. London: Kegan Paul, Trench, Trubner & Co.

Cleary, T. (1984). *The Flower Ornament Scripture: A Translation of The Avatamasaka Sutra*. Boston: Shambhala Publications.

Epstein, R. (2003). *Buddhism A to Z*. Burlingame: The Buddhist Text Translation Society.

Gethin, R. (1998). *The Foundations of Buddhism*. Oxford: Oxford University Press.

Hagen, S. (2012). *Why the World Doesn't Seem to Make Sense*. Boulder: Sentient Publications.

Herold, A. F. (1954). *The Life of Buddha: According to the Ancient Legends of India*. Tokyo: Charles E. Tuttle.

Holiday, B. (1939). *God Bless the Child*.

Jasanoff, J. H. (2002). "The Vedic Imperatives yodhi 'Fight' and bodhi 'Heed'." *Journal of the American Oriental Society*, 290–95.

Johnston, E. H. (1936). *Asvaghosa's Buddhacarita or Acts of the Buddha*. Lahore: Motilal Banarsidass.

Obeyesekere, R. (2009). *Yasodhara, the Wife of the Bodhisattva*. New York: State University of New York Press.

Pollan, M. (2013, May 19). "Some of My Best Friends Are Bacteria." *New York Times Sunday Magazine*, p. MM36.

Sahn, Z. M. (1997). *The Compass of Zen*. Boston: Shambhala Publications.

Suzuki, S. (1970). *Zen Mind, Beginner's Mind*. Boston: Shambhala Publications.

Thomas, E. J. (1927). *The Life of Buddha as Legend and History*. London: Routledge & Kegan Paul Ltd.

Watson, B. (1993). *The Zen Teachings of Master Lin-Chi*. New York: Columbia University Press.

ABOUT THE AUTHOR

 Anita Feng is a Zen master teaching at the Blue Heron Zen Community, Seattle, in the Korean lineage of Zen Master Seung Sahn. She is a writer and sculptor of original raku buddhas. She lives in Issaquah, Washington. Information about her books, sculpture, and Zen training can be found at golden-wind.com.

ABOUT THE ARTIST

 Linda Davidson is a Seattle, Washington-based fine artist and instructor who works primarily in drawing and painting media. For more information about her work, please visit lindadavidson.com.

ABOUT WISDOM PUBLICATIONS

Wisdom Publications is the leading publisher of classic and contemporary Buddhist books and practical works on mindfulness. Publishing books from all major Buddhist traditions, Wisdom is a nonprofit charitable organization dedicated to cultivating Buddhist voices the world over, advancing critical scholarship, and preserving and sharing Buddhist literary culture.

To learn more about us or to explore our other books, please visit our website at wisdompubs.org. You can subscribe to our eNewsletter, request a print catalog, and find out how you can help support Wisdom's mission either online or by writing to:

Wisdom Publications
199 Elm Street
Somerville, Massachusetts 02144 USA

You can also contact us at 617-776-7416 or info@wisdompubs.org.

Wisdom is a 501(c)(3) organization, and donations in support of our mission are tax deductible.

Wisdom Publications is affiliated with the Foundation for the Preservation of the Mahayana Tradition (FPMT).

ALSO AVAILABLE FROM WISDOM PUBLICATIONS

The World Is Made of Stories
David Loy

"Loy's book is like the self: layer after layer peels away, and the center is empty. But the pleasure is exactly in the exploration. At once Loy's most accessible and most philosophical work."
—Alan Senauke for *Buddhadharma*

Zen Encounters with Loneliness
Terrance Keenan

"Every few years, if you're lucky, a book comes along that changes your life. *Zen Encounters with Loneliness* is one of those books."—Satya Robyn, author of *Afterwards*